
★

THEY WERE SHREWDER THAN THEY LOOKED, THE COURTENAYS....

Venetia's eyes were alight with mischief as she leaned over and said to Kemp: "We're going to hire the manor out for parties where people can let their hair down. We might advertise it for orgies... Or a meeting-place for some of the weirder cults where everyone takes their clothes off."

The twins fell back together in paroxysms of clownish laughter which was in no way good-humoured. Kemp fought hard against growing temper, sensing he was the butt of their mockery. It made him more alert to the peculiar chemistry which seemed to work between them and accentuate their worst features. For the first time he thought of the Courtenay twins as quite dangerous.

★

"A style and grace that makes one think of P.D. James."

—Andrew Greeley

M.R.D. Meek has a "fine writing style and brilliant talent for plot."

—Mystery News

THIS BLESSED PLOT

M.R.D. MEEK

W🌐RLDWIDE®

TORONTO • NEW YORK • LONDON
AMSTERDAM • PARIS • SYDNEY • HAMBURG
STOCKHOLM • ATHENS • TOKYO • MILAN
MADRID • WARSAW • BUDAPEST • AUCKLAND

THIS BLESSED PLOT

A Worldwide Mystery/April 1992

This edition is reprinted by arrangement with Charles Scribner's Sons; an imprint of Macmillan Publishing Company.

ISBN 0-373-26093-8

THIS BLESSED PLOT

ONE

'JULIE SORRENTO? Is that correct?'

'Yeah. Mrs.'

'Sorrento. Like the place in Italy?'

'Huh?' She looked blank.

Kemp spelled it out.

'Yeah, that's right. Sorrento.'

She was not going to be an easy client. But Lennox Kemp had grown accustomed to all kinds, including the inarticulate. He looked across his desk at this one.

That she was female was only apparent in the roundness of the bosom under a greyish-white T-shirt which bore the legend 'I'm One of Them'—an advertisement sufficiently ambiguous to signify the whole human race or any small esoteric section of it. He didn't think it meant the Tory party, despite the blue lettering. His mother, a tidy lady who put soap before sensibility, would have sniffed and said: 'The Great Unwashed.'

And indeed Mrs Julie Sorrento had brought in with her the faint sour smell of unclean clothing along with two small children, a toddler of a girl now clinging to a chair leg, and a bigger boy of perhaps three years who was investigating the lock on the bottom drawer of the filing cabinet. For the moment he looked safe enough.

Kemp concentrated on Mrs Sorrento, trying to make out her features through the screen of pseudo-Rastafarian ringlets which snaked down from the tufted black fringe obscuring her forehead. He wondered what it must be like to live on the other side of that curtain of hair, peering out as little animals do in the undergrowth. But little animals have bright eyes; from all he could see of Julie Sorrento's they held neither light nor colour.

'The DHSS sent me. See if you could help. They said I'd have to get a solicitor... You was the nearest.' She didn't sound enthusiastic about either the Department for Social Security or himself.

'That's what we're here for,' said Kemp cheerfully, as if his words encompassed not only the firm of Gillorns, Solicitors, who employed him but by implication the entire English judiciary system. Almost automatically his hand strayed towards the holder for Legal Aid forms. 'Just what can I do for you, Mrs Sorrento?'

'Like they said, down at the Social Security. Find my husband.'

'Has he gone missing? For how long?'

As Kemp drew his notebook towards him he glanced casually at his watch for, even under Legal Aid, time is still money. He wondered what Mrs Sorrento did with her time. Probably spent it tending those kids—though to his admittedly inexpert eye they didn't look all that well-cared for. The little girl's frock had a trailing hem, the boy's dark face was pasty. Kemp didn't dare to turn around to look more closely because he sensed from the tinkling sound that young Sorrento had discovered paper-clips and could be eating them. Mrs Sorrento seemed indifferent to the presence of the children; perhaps she was so used to having them around that they had become merely items of furniture that moved.

Luciano Sorrento had not been seen by her for a week. They had been married four years and lived in a caravan at The Willows on what was once a gipsy encampment now sanitized, concreted over, and controlled by the Council. Luciano had come origi-nally from Sicily to work in the tomato houses, he had met Julie, bedded and wedded her, and now he was gone, leaving her destitute. No, she'd never worked since they got married—indeed she seemed horrified at the suggestion. 'Lucky didn't hold with it,' she said with a shake of her Medusa hair in ei-ther pride or disgust. 'Besides, I 'ad the kids, didn't I?'

'Indeed you did,' Kemp acknowledged hastily. 'Now, Mrs Sorrento, where do *you* think he's gone?' He stressed the pronoun, hoping for some lead, but her only answer was the predictable shrug.

'I dunno, do I? Or I wouldn't be here.'

'You must have some idea. Did you have a row with him?'

'Lots. He were no good.'

'In what sense?'

She stared at him—if anything as direct as a stare could find its way out from the tangle of black strands across her eyes.

'Kept me short, 'e did. Always goin' on about that allotment of his. Spent money on seed and the like, not on me...'

It appeared that the subject of Luciano's allotment had rankled.

'They took the plot back in the end, the Council did...for development, like.' She spat the words out with some satisfaction. 'Good riddance, I said.'

'I see,' said Kemp, who didn't, but he had to press on. 'Apart from his allotment, where does your husband work?'

'Down at Everetts. Nothing wrong with his wages there—what I ever got to see of them.'

Everetts were one of the largest of the tomato and cucumber growers in the Lea Valley and, so far as Kemp knew, they had an excellent record as employers.

'And what do they say at Everetts?'

Again the shrug. It was as if her T-shirt was made for it—the movement sent it slipping off and on her shoulders. 'Lucky never gave them no notice. Just went off, like.'

'So he wasn't sacked?'

'Naw. He was a good worker.' This, grudgingly. 'Foreman says Lucky just left the Friday night as usual and never came in the Monday.'

'And when he went to work that Friday morning was the last you saw of him?'

She nodded. It was nice to get affirmation of something, and Kemp got down to the task of eliciting further details, which proved as hard as trying to extract juice from a dry orange.

They were interrupted suddenly by a gurgling sound, and Mrs Sorrento gave a muffled shriek. Kemp swung his chair round and saw to his horror that the little boy was standing as if petrified, blood pouring from his wide-open mouth. As he raised reddened fingers to his face and clawed at his face they left scarlet streaks all down his cheeks.

'For God's sake!' Kemp's heart lurched in panic as he grabbed the boy and pulled him across to the desk. Something dropped to the ground, and a crimson stain spread over the carpet. Bereft of coherent thought, Kemp took hold of the boy's mouth and stared into it. Great floods of red were bubbling up inside and what looked like a welter of blood was spewing out and running down the chin.

Kemp's foot caught on the thing that had fallen. He looked down.

'Red ink!' he cried, in mingled relief and annoyance. 'He's drunk my bottle of red ink.'

He strode across to the door and flung it open. 'Elvira!' he shouted. 'I want you.'

Fortunately Elvira wasn't far away, and she came running. She'd never known Mr Kemp to get in such a state; he was usually such a calm person. But when she took one look at the boy, now screaming his head off, she very nearly screamed herself.

'It's only ink,' said Kemp, pushing young Sorrento not altogether gently into her arms. 'Please take the infant Dracula to the washroom and clean out his mouth.' He picked up the bottle. 'He's only had a spoonful as far as I can see, and judging from what came out he hasn't swallowed any. You too, Mrs Sorrento, you'd best go with the lad to make sure he's all right.'

He'd noticed she hadn't budged from her chair, and it was only with reluctance she got up and followed Elvira, who was already soothing the little boy. 'If you're good and do as I say,' she told him, 'I've got some orange juice in my room and lots of chocolate biscuits.'

The wailing subsided as the door closed, and Kemp found himself clutched by the trouser leg. Mother seemed to have forgotten her younger child who was gazing up with great brown eyes, a smudge of dirt on her nose. She appeared quite unconcerned about the exploit of her brother; perhaps she was used to this sort of thing. Kemp plumped her down in a chair at his desk with paper and a coloured pencil which she proceeded to press down until the point broke, so she sucked it instead. She was contented enough, however, and smiled winningly at Kemp. He got the impression that Maria, as she was called, was a stolid little girl and in the habit of being left to her own devices.

Elvira returned the mother after a few minutes. 'Luke's taken a fancy to my room,' she said, 'so just give him a shout when you're ready to leave, Mrs Sorrento.'

Kemp guessed the fancy had something to do with the offer of chocolate biscuits but he wasn't sorry to be deprived of young Luke's company, and he admired Elvira's adroitness—especially when she added, pointedly: 'And your next appointment's waiting downstairs, Mr Kemp.' He was beginning to get rather tired of the whole Sorrento family.

Not exactly a well-knit clan either, he thought, as his client seated herself again, taking no notice of the little girl whom he'd been amusing by teaching her to thread paperclips like a daisy chain. He couldn't help wondering just how Lucky Luciano had earned the name—certainly not through marriage.

'Lucky? Is that what you call him?'

'Sure. It's a lot easier than Luciano.' Even then she didn't pronounce the Italian name correctly. Funny, after four years of wedlock, but from what Kemp had gleaned of Julie Sorrento she probably hadn't bothered to learn.

'And was he ever lucky?' Kemp asked, on a whim.

For the first time a spark of what might be construed as intelligence gleamed in the dullness of her eyes.

'He's supposed to have won a bit in a lottery in Italy a while back. Least that's what Alfredo told him. Alfredo's his brother. He come over on holiday. Said he'd taken the ticket for Lucky and it come up, like.' It was a long sentence for her but, as with all her utterances, not a model of clarity.

'You mean Alfredo brought the money over?'

'Some of it. It didn't amount to much, anyway, and Lucky spent it all on wine.'

'Your husband drank a lot?'

'Like a fish.' The admission didn't seem to bother her, which surprised Kemp, for most of the Italian workers he'd come across were sober and hard-working. 'But you'll know all about Alfredo's holi-day,' she went on. 'It was done proper like, in here.'

She looked round Kemp's room as if he'd only to open a cabinet and all would be revealed. It slowly dawned on him what she meant.

'You mean the papers in connection with Al-fredo's holiday were prepared here in Gillorns? My dear Mrs Sorrento, that may well be so but I can as-sure you I didn't deal with the matter or I would have remembered the name.'

If Alfredo Sorrento had come on a visit to his rel-atives they would have had to give the usual assur-ance to the authorities that they would maintain him in their home for the duration of his stay, and not let him run around loose, sneaking a job away from a good British working man, or landing penniless on the State.

'When did your brother-in-law Alfredo come over?'

She was vague; time was not something she dealt with easily.

'Can't remember offhand. Last month it'd be. Yeah, in July.'

It seemed a shame to strain her memory further. If it was going to be relevant, Kemp could always check up the papers in the office. It did look to him possible that the two brothers had concocted some scheme whereby Julie's husband might skip off to Italy for the rest of the lottery money. It was a reasonable assumption, but if he'd stayed there in the land of his birth any hope of getting maintenance out of him for her and the children would be doomed.

To put this suggestion baldly to Mrs Sorrento would bring an hysterical outburst of tears of rage, and on this stuffy August afternoon when he was feeling pretty tired himself Kemp didn't think he could cope with either—nor the effect on the little girl now exploring the floor under his desk.

It was not that he lacked compassion, but he had had his fill of such cases; erring husbands who shirked their responsibilities, leaving their families on the breadline; the men's whereabouts had to be traced, summonses issued which would inevitably be disregarded, the long tedious haul through the courts, a waste of time and emotion.

He was conscious of his mood, and irritated by it as much as by the way she slouched in her chair, the dirty fingernails, the stale smell of her clothes. She wasn't even interesting as a woman...

He pulled himself together. She had come as a client, and as a client she must be treated.

THERE WERE TIMES Kemp could summon up resources of patience beyond the call of duty, and certainly outside the confines of Legal Aid. He had to draw on these resources now to complete his interview with Mrs Sorrento but eventually from the bits and pieces she reluctantly let through her nicotine-stained teeth he was able to come up with some kind of coherent story.

Alfredo Sorrento had come for a fortnight in July under the relatives' visiting scheme, and had then returned to the family home in Sicily.

'Yeah. Alfredo was OK. He was no hassle.'

'Did the brothers get on?'

'Sure. You know what these Italians are like.'

Kemp didn't, but assumed she had the experience.

'Yeah, Alfredo brought some of the lottery money. Not all of it, not by a long chalk.'

'Then, is it not possible,' Kemp suggested, gently, 'that your husband has gone to Sicily to get the rest of it?'

She stared at him glumly as though such an idea would never cross her mind.

'Huh?'

'Perhaps Alfredo suggested it?'

'But Lucky'd have told me. I mean, going off like that...' Her mouth turned down. 'The bastard.' It was said without anger, more a weary acceptance.

'In the meantime, did he leave you any money?'

''Course not. He and Alfredo spent what they'd got. I'm not sayin' they didn't take us all out for trips, like. Anyways, it's all gone. Why'd you think I've been down to the bloody DHSS? Maintenance for me and the kids, that's what they said, that's what I oughter have.'

'I see.' It was plain enough, although discouraging, to say the least. 'But you do realize we can hardly serve a maintenance summons on your husband when we don't know where he is?'

Kemp gave her the unpalatable truth as, with sinking heart, he already knew what her answer would be.

'Well, it'll be your job to find him, won't it? That's what they told me down the road. Said you'd got the know-how, like.'

Like passing the buck. Kemp sighed. More questions, and inadequate answers. He took notes which were scrappy, then got to his feet and disengaged Maria's clinging fingers from his in-tray.

'You go back to those good ladies at the Social Services,' he said, more heartily than he felt, 'and get them to give you payments to tide you and the children over. Any benefits can be paid back by your husband in due course—when we find him. And that's my job, as you so nicely put it.'

The small sarcasm was wasted on her and he was rather ashamed of using it on so poor a creature.

'Would you mind signing this Legal Aid form?' He passed it over to her along with his ballpoint pen. 'It means I can pursue inquiries as to your husband's whereabouts.'

She scraped back some of the curtain of hair, and looked suspiciously at the form.

'Hey, this won't get me into no trouble, will it? Lucky's against me signing things.'

'No trouble, I assure you.'

She scrawled 'J. Sorrento' where he showed her on the form, and handed it back.

'It's like he's from Sicily,' she observed darkly. 'He told me you gotta be careful out there because of the Mafia.'

'This is England, Mrs Sorrento,' Kemp told her, severely, startled in spite of himself. 'We don't have the Mafia over here...'

With all the other futilities looming ahead in this inquiry, scant information to go on and a witless client, Kemp felt he needed the Mafia like a hole in the head. There had been plenty of Italians around the Lea Valley for years now and, apart from introducing a kind of feudal strip system in dividing fields between families, none of them had reverted to more dangerous Sicilian mores, and few fell foul of the law except for liking fast cars and disdaining speed limits.

Mrs Sorrento had got up and was pulling at her tight cotton skirt. She put out an unseeing hand for the child, Maria, who went to her without enthusiasm still clutching her coloured pencil.

Kemp opened the door for them, and called to Elvira that it was time to reunite the family. He caught a whiff of cheap scent from the greasy tangle of black hair as Julie Sorrento slouched past. She'd be taller than me if only she straightened herself up, he thought. Being of middle stature himself, he was conscious of height in others. Her legs weren't bad, either.

When Elvira showed in his next client she said, with a disapproving sniff: 'I had to wash my hands, Mr Kemp. That little boy's clothes!'

LATER IN THE AFTERNOON, Kemp pulled the telephone towards him and set about making the routine calls that might or might not lead to the errant Lucky Luciano Sorrento being found and made aware of his responsibilities towards his sluttish wife and two tousled kids. Kemp rang the local employers, the employment exchange, the Council, and, as an afterthought, his good friend Sergeant Cobbins at the Police Station.

At the end of an hour he had gained nothing but frustration.

The manager of Everetts confirmed that Mr Sorrento was missing—so far as his work in the tomato houses was concerned; they were not interested in his domestic shortcomings. If Mr Kemp cared to call, yes, he could talk to other employees but he wouldn't get much help from them, Sorrento having been a taciturn chap even with his fellow Italians.

No, the labour exchange were not aware he was out of work, nor had he sought benefit. Yes, they would make inquiries, but you know those foreign workers, they tend to go from job to job as if they'd never read the rules—well, possibly some of them couldn't . . .

Yes, the rates on the caravan were paid up to date. Why was Mr Kemp asking? Was there going to be a difficulty? Knowing the rating officials' sensitivity about possible matrimonial troubles, Kemp fielded that one.

No, Sorrento had never been in contact with the police nor they with him. As for other law-abiding citizens, his name was unknown to them. Why was Mr Kemp looking for him? Like the rating officer, Detective-Sergeant Cobbins kept a weather eye skinned for clouds on the horizon. A problem of maintenance payments? That's your pitch, pal—not in such terms, but the meaning was clear.

Kemp looked at the photograph Julie had produced out of the mess of cosmetics, children's toys, chocolate bars and what looked like pants, from her sling-bag. It was a rather unsatisfactory snapshot taken in what looked like deep undergrowth on a gloomy day, out of focus and from a distance. The figure could have been any man between twenty and forty in a boilersuit, leaning on a spade, but it was all she said she had. The Sorrentos hadn't gone in for photography much.

There had been quite an influx of Italian visitors coming to see their relatives that summer—Alfredo Sorrento's form was just one of many and gave scant information beyond the address on the caravan site at The Willows, and the length of his stay. Nobody in the office at Gillorns could recall who had come in about it. 'They all look alike to me,' said Peter Carruthers, the cashier, as if he was talking about orientals, 'dark-skinned and no speaka da English. I think this form was filled in by the young temporary law clerk we had at the time. You know, the one who's gone off to the States for a better job. Not that he'd have been much use to you—he'd have forgotten his own name if it hadn't been emblazoned on his briefcase in letters of gold. If that's what they call the brain-drain, then I'm all for it.'

Before going home that night Kemp phoned the DHSS. Yes, Mrs Sorrento had gone back to them. Yes, the voice went on, acidly, they would do what they could. It didn't sound as if Mrs Sorrento was their favourite client either.

TWO

LETTICE WARRENDER was laughing at one of Kemp's jokes. This she found easy to do since she had known him for some time and was well past any dangerous tendency to fall in love with him.

'The only reason you're calling the Newtown Development Corporation a branch of the Mafia is because you've just lost that planning appeal,' she told him with mocking severity.

'I didn't lose it. My client did,' Kemp corrected her.

'Well, I'm glad he didn't get his monstrous high-rise apartment block. It would have ruined the skyline.'

'My dear girl, that skyline was ruined long ago. It was beyond redemption from the moment your lot turned the first sod.'

By 'your lot' he meant the Corporation which employed her, and in which she had already attained a position of some power by combining youthful idealism with a hard conservative common sense inherited from land-owning forbears, now down on their uppers as she was rising on hers.

Lettice and Kemp amicably agreed to differ on whether the vast conglomerate that Newtown had become was a true realization of the Utopian vision of its creators or a sprawling mess of random buildings, every one of which cheerfully embraced all the architectural heresies known to man, and the whole place only held together by yellow no-parking lines.

Kemp was kicking his heels in her office deep within the bowels of the first—and possibly the worst—of these, the flagship of the Corporation's fleet. She was serving him coffee in a cardboard cup.

'I wanted to ask you a favour, Lennox.'

'Surely it ought to be the other way round. We're the ones supposed to bribe officials.'

'Don't be silly. It's got nothing to do with work.'

'Then it's granted.'

'You're very trusting. Are you doing anything on Saturday night?'

'Even if I was, I'd drop it for you, Letty. Are you taking me out?'

'Sort of. You know John is away in Sweden?' Lettice had recently become engaged. 'Well, I've had an invitation to a party on Saturday...'

'Say no more. I'm your man if you're looking for an uncle-figure as escort. Safe, elderly but not yet senile...'

'Come off it, Lennox, you're not that many years over forty.'

'Too many for anyone to get improper ideas about us—much as I would like them to. Anyway, where is this party?'

'Do you know the Courtenays?'

'If you mean personally, of course I don't. I'm not in that league. Don't they speak only to royalty?'

'So you have heard of them?'

'Hasn't everyone? You mean this "do" is at their place? At Courtenay Manor? You surprise me, Lettice, the circles you move in.'

He looked around the grey office, at the sternly functional steel cabinets, the drably-painted walls.

She grinned.

'I know what you're getting at, Lennox, but my life has been full of such contrasts. I like it that way. There's Castleton House—getting pretty threadbare I'm afraid—on the one hand, and on the other—this.'

The Warrender family had not been pleased when Lettice opted for polytechnic college and a career instead of being properly finished in Switzerland and marriage to someone of her own class.

'I was at Benenden with Venetia Courtenay. She was a bit ahead of me in the school but she rather took me up in the way clever, attractive girls do with the plainer, plodding kind.' Lettice could afford to smile complacently at the memory. 'And of course we were near neighbours at home, although the Courtenays were always far more "County" that we could ever afford to be.'

'Isn't she married?'

'Oh yes, to some dim little stockbroker called Proby but she still likes to call herself Courtenay— the name's too precious to lose entirely. And Proby doesn't count for much either to her or to the City as far as I can gather. He's been no more successful playing the money game than my dear old Dad.'

It was Kemp's turn to smile. He was pleased that Lettice could take a lenient view of her father; shares recommended by Lionel Warrender tended to go down like lead balloons. He lacked the flair, and would have done better to have stayed home and farmed his diminishing acres. All the same, he'd not done badly out of the Development Corporation which had built on them. Courtenay Manor was another story. Too far out, and its agricultural land too rich, it had been left untouched in all its feudal magnificence.

'This party. . . is it to be a grand affair?' he asked nervously. 'I'm not really up to that sort of thing...'

'I'm not sure that I am either, Lennox. It's ages since I saw Venetia, and she's probably only asked me for old time's sake. She and her brother, Vivian, have been knocking around the world on the cheap these last few years. Waiting to come into their inheritance, I suppose. Now that old Uncle Silas has died at last, this'll be a celebration.'

'How cynical you young folk are! Silas Courtenay was only buried a week or two ago.'

'Well, he was over ninety. They'd had a long wait. Coming back to the point, it's not the sort of thing I'd want to go to on my own. Venetia and Vivian always had a lot of smart friends even when they'd no money...'

'But they had expectations,' said Kemp drily. 'Smart people would feel the gravitational pull.'

'Now who's being cynical? Anyway, it might be fun seeing how the rich and noble squander their time. Funny to think of the twins coming into all that. Of course they were always so haughty about the Courtenay name but now there's the money as well there'll be no holding them . . .'

'I didn't know they were twins.'

'Oh yes, Venetia and Vivian were born within the hour, and have been inseparable ever since. Her marriage wouldn't be allowed to interfere with that.'

'Venetia and Vivian Courtenay,' Kemp mused. 'Sounds like something out of a Victorian novel. By Lord Lytton, perhaps, or Disraeli. I read them avidly when I was young just for the high-sounding names. I never really cottoned on to what they were all about but I do remember to this day how Vivian Grey gave a loud shriek and fell on the lifeless body of Violet Fane!'

'And you've been falling over lifeless bodies ever since. You're famous for it . . .'

This sweeping allusion, though not inaccurate, nevertheless rankled with Lennox Kemp. Of late he had been thinking it was high time he refurbished that image, and became the very model of the steady conscientious solicitor his firm had the right to expect instead of indulging his own whim, playing detective and chasing murderers.

'Not any more,' he said, firmly, 'I'm a reformed character. Next time I find a lifeless body I'm going to ignore it. Anyway, some of that notoriety you speak of has been too perilously gained. It's the quiet life for me from now on.'

Lettice looked at him with affection. He looked quiet enough, chubby and unassuming, like a rather worn teddy-bear, but looks could be deceptive. She knew he had a sharp brain and a critical eye, and that he accepted no one at their own valuation. It would be interesting to see what he would make of the Courtenay twins who put such a high price upon their name and lineage that their personal qualities had never been challenged.

IT WAS a mixed gathering of persons, both as to dress and social status, that assembled under the chandeliers of the great hall and drawing-room at the Manor on Saturday evening. Lettice was relieved to see a few Newtown notables, a couple of young clerics, a doctor she recognized, and Amy Francis, the owner of the local riding school.

Mrs Blanche Courtenay was graciousness itself although her greeting had been vague: 'You're the little Warrender girl…' She pronounced it 'gurl'. 'And is your dear mother well? I must call some time… Mr Kemp. Are you from Newtown?' She made it sound like a Council estate. 'Oh, with Gillorns? I knew Archie once… a long time ago. Retired? Ah, well, things do change…' She went on her way with a slight weaving movement, a rather incongruous figure in chiffon draperies. She was possibly the oldest person present.

'The mother,' whispered Lettice succinctly. 'A fine seat on a horse—and that was about the only thing she was attached to for long, they used to say... Hullo, Amy, do you know a lot of people here?'

'No, I don't.' Amy Francis was an athletic-looking woman in her forties with a weatherbeaten face and steady blue eyes. 'They're mostly friends of Viv's— and Venetia's, of course. Have you seen the terrible twins yet? They're holding court in the drawing-room.'

'Were they ever pupils of yours, Mrs Francis?' Kemp asked. He had dealt with some of her legal problems and admired her businesslike approach to them. Many found her too brusque and plain-spoken for their liking but in Kemp's profession, where time was ever-increasingly being equated with money, her ability to grasp a point counted for more than glib courtesies.

'No, thank God. They disrupted quite enough educational establishments in their youth, but fortunately they never took to horses—or perhaps it was the other way round. They were a disappointment to their Mama in that respect, as in others... What are you doing here, Mr Kemp?' Her question meant no incivility. She was not one to beat around the bush. 'Concerned in the famous trust, are you?'

'I sincerely hope not. I think Mr Archie Gillorn may still be one of the trustees, but anyway these things are dealt with at our London office.'

'Old money,' Amy Francis commented, with some satisfaction. 'Blanche told me about it once. All neatly tied up so that the rats couldn't get at it... Until now, of course.'

Kemp watched her take a glass from a passing tray. It had not been her first. He followed her example.

'Old money's the same as new,' he said. 'It can only be spent.'

'Silas Courtenay didn't believe in spending. He was a hoarder, that's why there's so much of it. Now it'll all go on this kind of romp.'

The old-fashioned word made Kemp murmur: 'The elegant stupidity of private parties. That was Jane Austen's view of them.'

Amy gave out a contemptuous sound—something between a neigh and a snort. 'Not much elegance about this one. The young people in there are real rag, tag and bobtail.' She waved her glass in the direction of one of the rooms where shrieks of laughter cut through the rumble of heavy rock music and the pounding of feet.

'The Pony Club at practice?' Kemp hazarded, with a smile.

'Not on your life. More like the hordes of Bacchus.'

Kemp relinquished Amy to a man in tweed and cavalry twill, an outfit inappropriate to a warmish evening but not significantly so, since dress on this occasion seemed to be so optional as to include every concession to personal whim. Smooth backs and satin straps, flounced shirts and velvet drainpipes, skinny jeans and mohair sweaters, suede jerkins and metal-studded jackets, brocade waistcoats and Peruvian ponchos, it was difficult to sort out male from female.

Kemp drifted, looking for Lettice who had bounded off earlier towards the drawing-room. He passed a group who had settled themselves on cushions in a corner. The girls had spiky Afro hairstyles and padded shoulders, swathed in dark brown fake furs which glistened in the lights. With their long black-ribbed legs stretched out in front of them they looked like a family of little gorillas admiring their toes. Small furry animals lurking in the undergrowth; he was reminded of Julie Sorrento and passed on, grinning to himself.

There was a calmer air through the arch, and it was cooler. It was a great green-and-white room, gold only decorously placed around the uncurtained windows and touching here and there the top of a vase, the edge of a mirror. It was a room of restrained elegance, the more so for the absence of ostentation except perhaps for the elaborate plaster ceiling, too lofty for casual sight. Kemp's eyes were drawn upwards. From the central lozenge the ancient arms of the Courtenays looked down with proud indifference as they probably had for centuries on the activities of their name-bearers. He wondered if Silas the Gatherer had bothered much about the coat of arms—that reward of some merchant ancestor's profitable flirtation with the fickle Tudor dynasty.

There was no mistaking the present holders of the name. Vivian and Venetia Courtenay were ranged on either side of the enormous mantelpiece as though they were sufficient ornament for its rather empty grandeur. Which, up to a point, they were. Both were tall, spare of frame, with high-held heads and an air of always being in the right place at the right time. She had beautiful shoulders and a neck so white and shapely the Victorians would have called it swan-like.

Each of the Courtenays had a coterie of people around them, among whom, on Venetia's side Kemp glimpsed Lettice Warrender. She seemed to have been looking out for him, for almost immediately she hurried over.

'I do want you to meet Venetia,' she said, almost dragging him towards the fireplace as if he were some kind of prize exhibit.

There was a small space in front of Venetia as there might be between a queen and her respectful subjects, and indeed Kemp did have the sensation of being presented at court.

The illusion was quickly dashed by Venetia herself. She had listened impatiently, tapping a silver-shod foot on the stone hearth, as Lettice stumbled through the proper form of introduction to finish lamely: '... and this is Lennox Kemp...'

'Of course it is, Letty. Didn't I ask you to bring him? I'm so glad you could come, Lennox.'

Kemp glanced at Lettice. Her face had reddened. Unlike her to get so flustered about mere civilities.

'I told you my fiancé was away,' she muttered to Venetia, keeping her eyes from Kemp.

'How very *alt-modisch* of you to have a fiancé! I thought they'd gone out with dirndl skirts... And I said why don't you bring along that nice Mr Kemp.'

Observing the by-play, nice Mr Kemp remained silent till Venetia Courtenay turned to him and gave him the full treatment from clear silvery-grey eyes that held a tinge of green. But perhaps that was only reflection from the painted walls.

'You see, Lennox,' she said, 'now that Vivian and I have come into our own we want to get to know everyone of note in Newtown.'

'That is a wide scope. By what criteria?'

'Do we assess notability?' She was quick to take his meaning. 'Why, the broadest view. Let them all come and we will sort them out. You, I understand, have made quite a name for yourself...'

'In what capacity? I go about very little in Newtown society. I play neither golf nor bridge, nor do I ride to hounds. Are you sure you've got the right man?' If she wanted to play the grande dame with words it amused him to join, and match her.

Kemp's eyes, too, were grey but vacuous and opaque compared with hers. Lettice, watching them, thought they were like a pair of fencers warily sizing each other up, and she wondered again why Venetia had insisted she bring him to this party, why the idiotic subterfuge, and why, oh why, after all these years could Venetia still reduce her to a fumbling schoolgirl?

Venetia suddenly broke off her conversation with Kemp—a conversation which seemed to him contrived and essentially trivial yet which held a disturbing undercurrent—and called out: 'Vivian? Do come and meet Mr Lennox Kemp.'

'Ah, our local sleuth.' Vivian Courtenay put an arm around his sister's neck in a gesture at once brotherly and possessive. He placed his glass carefully on a console table and held out a hand to Kemp. He had a strong grip at variance with his languid stance. Like many tall slender men, he had the slightly unbalanced look of a willow tree.

'If the only fame your sister assigns to me is that, then I'd have no honest clients.' Kemp smiled up at Vivian Courtenay, whose eyes he noticed were grey as hers but smaller, darker and totally devoid of any saving humour.

'Could we not pass as honest clients?' said Venetia, with a pout someone must have told her was delicious. 'Vivian has great plans for the estate. Sports activities, a leisure centre, the kind of lark... What would you say to the Manor as a fun-palace?'

'I would say you have already opened,' said Kemp, as a throng of dishevelled dancers burst into the room, scattering the pale Chinese rugs and sliding on

the bare boards they had only half-heartedly covered.

Venetia clapped her hands. 'A Conga, a Conga,'
she cried. 'I do so love a Conga...'

She skipped away into the midst of them, and was
soon gathered up in the crowd, a flying figure in her
short glittery sheath, the blonde hair so carefully
coiled up now loose about her shoulders. It was a
surprising transformation to Kemp who had thought
her statuesque and cold as the marble mantel against
which she had stood. Not so to Lettice Warrender
who had known Venetia of old, one moment the
haughty sixth-former too aloof to bother with small
fry, the next a madcap leader of young disreputa-
bles, a breaker of rules, a hatcher of hare-brained
schemes...

'That London rabble...' There was sneering dismissal in Vivian's tone. 'We'll soon get rid of them.'
He drew Kemp aside with an almost imperious grasp
on his arm. 'Seriously, Kemp, we could use a good
solicitor in Newtown to cut through all this dead
wood in their planning. No disrespect to you, Lettice old thing...'

Kemp disengaged himself adroitly without actually brushing off the other's hand. He was never
quite at ease with tall men, he could not watch the
movement in their eyes and their height unnerved
him.

'Pleased to have met you, Mr Courtenay,' he said
in the American style which was not his own, and

stressing the 'Mr' which the other man had dropped
in addressing himself—bad manners, in Kemp's
view, on such short acquaintance. Vivian Courtenay
was a puppy—possibly the new breed of yuppy-
puppy now that he had money to his name, but a
puppy nevertheless.

'I'm failing my protégée in not finding her some
supper,' he said lightly, steering Lettice away from
the group.

'You didn't like Vivian,' she murmured as they
crossed the floor.

'Was it so obvious?'

'Well, you didn't show the deference he expects—
he's always expected. Was it an instinctive dislike?'

Pushing his way through an off-shoot of the main
Conga—by the sound of it now rampaging through
the upper galleries—Kemp drew breath to consider.

'It has become a convention of the modern detective novel that dislikeable characters are not necessarily villains,' he observed sententiously, 'whereas
the nicest of people can, and often do, commit murder.'

'I could commit murder for a sandwich,' said
Lettice. 'I'm starving. There's supposed to be some
sort of spread in the dining-room.'

'If we can find it,' complained Kemp as someone
stepped on his foot. A tray of filled glasses appeared
at his elbow, and he took one for himself and passed
one to Lettice. 'Anyway,' he went on, warming to his
theme, 'in my profession one should never go on first

impressions, clients tend to go all fidgety and fishy when faced with lawyers, or they try the high-handed stuff like your Vivian, simply to assert themselves.'

'You do realize only champagne cocktails have been served here tonight?' Lettice eyed him with some suspicion; he was not usually so loquacious. 'I hope you've a strong head.'

'No stronger than most. That's why we'll get a minicab home whenever you're ready.'

'What, no golden carriage—not even a pumpkin? I'm not leaving till I've had something to eat. The dining-room's through that alcove, down the corridor next to the green baize door.'

'Behind which, no doubt, the servants are immured,' muttered Kemp, following her lead. The Great Hall now seemed not so much crowded as over-populated. People had taken to the walls, the outer corners and all the way up the vast staircase where they vanished into obscurity, while vague sounds of scuffling signalled more or less happy couplings in the higher reaches.

The dining-room, when they finally emerged into it, must have been in the eye of the storm for it was bleakly hushed. It had a gaunt, unused aspect not helped by dark oak-panelled walls to which not much attention appeared to have been given in recent years, and it was but dimly lit by an ironwork chandelier resembling the Crown of Thorns. Beneath this, the mother of the twins was sitting by the long table picking at the ruins of a cake whose colourful fondant icing had run, almost obscuring the hopeful message: 'Welcome Home'. In this context Mrs Courtenay looked like Miss Havisham, rather sprucer but not by much.

She raised a hand to Lettice and Kemp as faces she recognized, and bade them eat. Lettice took a plate hungrily, noting that the expense spared on the food bore no relation to that devoted to liquid refreshment—quantities of which were still on offer. At the other, more crowded end of the table champagne corks were popping and wine was being slurped into waiting glasses as though the evening was yet young and there was no tomorrow.

Beside Mrs Courtenay was a man whom Kemp immediately recognized with some surprise, but on an instant's thought, with acceptance of the inevitable. Arnold Crayshaw, old Archie Gillorn's successor in the London office.

The two eyed each other, as lawyers will, with the same instinctive wariness: What brings you here? Fortunately for Kemp, who had drunk more than it was his custom to do—thinking this a social occasion when he didn't need to have all his wits about him—it seemed that Arnold too had fully indulged. His large fleshy features were flushed, and his usually sharp eyes somewhat bloodshot.

'Hullo, Lennox. Didn't expect to see you here, but of course Newton's your patch these days.'

'I'm escorting Miss Warrender,' said Kemp firmly, to put a stop to any speculation. He introduced them.

'H'm. Know your father, young lady...' Arnold turned to his neighbour, a darkish man in pin-stripes, narrow for the shirt, broad for the suit. Looks like he's behind bars, thought Kemp, who was starting to feel quite merry. 'You know Lionel Warrender,' Arnold was saying, 'don't you, Lewis?'

Mrs Courtenay took a hand at the party game of further introductions: 'My son-in-law, Lewis Proby.' She didn't sound enthusiastic.

Kemp nodded politely and helped himself to a sausage-roll. Something grated between his teeth as he bit, confirming his suspicions; he knew those caterers in Newtown, cheap and not entirely reliable.

'Sit down here next to me, Mr Kemp.' Mrs Blanche Courtenay might have the appearance of a decayed gentlewoman but one could see from where her daughter had inherited her peremptory ways. Kemp relinquished his roll, sat down on the proffered chair and concentrated on the glass in his hand which someone seemed to have filled with quite a decent white wine.

'Now that I've got a brace of legal eagles at my table,' continued Mrs Courtenay, with mischief in her eye, 'you can put your heads together over my problem. Go off and play somewhere else, Proby, this isn't for your ears.' Though slightly slurred in the delivery, it was quite a speech, and Mr Proby was obviously used to the manner of it for he rose and joined Lettice now happily eating further up the table.

With this shift in the grouping Kemp realized that the twins' mother had effectively isolated himself and Arnold Crayshaw from any help by passing revellers. It was clear that had been her intention. Both pairs of lawyers' eyes met across the table in synchronized alarm.

'Not now, Blanche. Not the time, nor the place...' Crayshaw leaned forward and patted her arm.

'Nonsense, Arnold.' Mrs Courtenay plucked an iced pink rosette off the top of the cake, and popped it into her mouth, licking her fingers afterwards. 'I have to think of the gee-gees, you know.'

Crayshaw had a full, bubbling glass in front of him. He raised it, and drank the full contents in one long gulp. Kemp followed his example, and swallowed a draught of his wine in much the same spirit. If we both get drunk enough, he thought, we can slip to the floor and lie deader than the Statute of Mortmain.

Mrs Courtenay, however, was not to be deterred. She, after all, was only eating cake, and if she'd been drinking earlier in the evening she'd sobered since then, certainly enough to know what she wanted from both of them, and that was to talk about what she referred to as the bloody trust.

'You see, Mr Kemp,' she said, turning watery pale eyes on him, 'it's all turned out so unfair, and never what was meant. Archie'd never have left me poor as a churchmouse without a roof to my name...'

'You've the Dower House...' Arnold Crayshaw tried to get a word in.

'Yes,' said Kemp, not to be undone, 'that's what Dower Houses were for, provision for the widows...' He supposed Blanche to be a widow since no Courtenay father had been seen or mentioned. He realised that he was talking in the dark but felt he had to keep his end up when it came to legal issues.

'I don't want the bloody Dower House unless I can sell it on the open market and get a fancy price.'

'You can't sell a Dower House!' Crayshaw's horror at the suggestion won through his alcoholic haze. 'It's part of the estate.'

'Then get it off the estate. I need the capital if I'm to go in with Amy Francis. Ain't that what trustees are for, to raise capital?'

Despite the bubbles rising in his brain as exuberantly as they had done in his numerous drinks, Kemp could see a point when it was presented to him. He knew that the Francis Riding School wanted to expand but was short of capital; it seemed that Blanche Courtenay would like to be part of the venture.

'Couldn't she get a loan on it?' he asked tentatively—and stupidly, he quickly realized, when Arnold glared at him.

''Course she can't. She don't own it. She's only a tenant-for-life, as you might say.'

'Tenant, tenant! That's all I ever heard under this trust thing...' There was a near-tearful note in Blanche's voice. 'Silas was just a tenant for life, and look what a fortune he made! What's the difference? I thought tenants were just folks who had leases...'

Crayshaw staggered to his feet and grasped at a nearby bottle of wine. He held it out shakily over the lady's glass while Kemp's remaining intellectual powers tried wildly to get to grips with the unexplainable. No way in his present happy state of inebriation would he have been able to distinguish for the benefit of a lay client the difference between the inferior position of a holder for a term of years and the rightful owner, under a Settled Land Act trust, of the legal estate. Arnold Crayshaw didn't even try. 'Have some wine, Blanche,' he said, thickly, 'and we'll talk about this another time.'

'I don't want any wine. I want to talk about the Trust. Why was Silas this tenant thing you're always going on about?'

'Because that's how the Trust was set up. No one ever expected him to live so long, least of all himself... Just as no one expected your Charles to die before he came into his inheritance. But you know all that, Blanche.' Arnold gave a weary sigh, and slumped back into his chair.

'Charles... Poor Charles... Nobody remembers Charles...' Blanche evidently did for she began quietly to weep, at the same time stretching out her hand for her glass as though she needed solace. 'And now there's Venetia badgering me about him . . .'

'Charles?' Kemp raised an inquiring eyebrow at Arnold.

'Her husband. Died way back in 'forty-six. Shooting in Scotland. Got killed, going too fast round a bend in Appin. It all happened a long time ago. Blanche—' he put a podgy hand on her arm— 'I'll phone you tomorrow. We'll work something out. Now I've got to get home.' He lumbered slowly to his feet, holding fast to the table. 'I'll call a cab.'

'You actually know where there's a telephone in this palace?' Kemp, too, had risen, his head swimming. 'I'll bet it's gold-plated. Just show me . . .'

He managed to make the call, and collected Lettice who was by now as anxious to leave the party as he was. 'The food was terrible, the champagne lovely, the company indescribable,' she murmured sleepily as they waited for their transport on the steps of the portico—an unfortunate anachronism which did nothing for the rest of the building but at least gave some shelter from the rain which fell steadily without respect for departing guests.

Kemp soon spotted Bill Jenkins. Bill had taken to minicab-driving in the spirit of enterprise demanded by the new decade. When Margaret Thatcher had marched into Downing Street three years ago and said there was work to be done he hadn't agreed with her politics but he had taken the point. It was now 1982, and by such moonlighting activities many

Newtown workers like him were hoping not only to keep up with the high-spending times but even to prosper instead of merely struggling to survive as they had done throughout the bleak 'seventies.

Bill Jenkins wasn't much impressed by the feudal acres of Courtenay Manor but he was certainly put out by the lateness of the call.

'It's one o'clock in the morning, Mr Kemp,' he said as he drove away, blithely ignoring the many calls for lifts from benighted party-goers unfit to take charge of their own vehicles. 'I don't know what Elvira's going to say...'

Elvira, his wife, was Lennox Kemp's secretary, brought out some years ago from the urban wilderness of Walthamstow to the even wilder shores of Newtown.

'Tell her we were both working late.'

'That's a laugh, mate. You've been out on a binge, you and Miss Warrender here, but at least she hasn't drunk as much as you.' Not being directly employed by Gillorns, Bill had no need to show respect.

Lettice giggled.

'What were you in cahoots with Mother Courtenay and Mr Crayshaw about?'

'Something I wish to have nothing whatsoever to do with, now or at any future time...'

Kemp went to sleep. He should have been asleep hours ago.

THREE

SUNDAY MORNING in Newtown. There weren't
enough old churches left, nor new ones yet built, for
a carillon of bells to herald the Sabbath so it was left
to industrial inertia and nature's soft touch to give it
cognizance. A fine mist left over from last night's
rain clothed the jagged skyline with decent blue veil-
ing, and crept along the empty streets like a benign
visitor.

Kemp decided to walk out to the Manor to retrieve his car. It was more than five miles but he
needed the exercise. He had not been pleased with his
part in the goings-on of the previous night, and had
decided that champagne should be restricted to
weddings and that, when laced with brandy, it was a
tipple to be avoided.

The dews of morning cleared his head. The roads
were quiet, the hedgerows wreathed in spiders' webs,
each leaf and twig brought into their finely spun
structures. The snail's on the thorn, all's right with
the world . . . Kemp breathed deeply. An unpeopled
landscape was a rare thing.

He was no great walker, nor did he look it in an old
jacket and well-worn trousers. He was a townsman
without hiking boots of padded anorak, but he had

endurance and once started in an easy stroll he could go on for many miles. When clear of Newtown, and out into the green countryside where the fields lay at peace, untouched by the wilful hand of developers, he contemplated the rolling acres with a benevolent eye.

This was the very land of England, the essence of the soil itself, and the source of its most enduring laws; it had survived the feudal follies of kings, the twists and turns by which Equity curtailed the regal power, the greed of the great landowners, the turbulence of the Enclosure Acts, and the striving of the common people to assert their rights. Could it really escape in these new entrepreneurial times? He thought of leisure parks, and shuddered.

Because his mind was wandering, yet apt to alight on a subject recently spoken of, he considered the Trust, that peculiarly English concept which, once it had fought its way out of the thickets of feudalism, separated the actual ownership of the land from its beneficial interest, the rents and profits of its use. And what an admirable word that 'use' was— whether derived from the Roman *usus usufructas*, ancient Teutonic practice, or, as Maitland claimed, from the old Common Law rules of agency—that invention of wily lawyers which was to prove Chancery's gain. All academic now, of course... But land—this green and brown stuff he was actually seeing—and the use to which it was put had always been central to English law, and flowed over into every modern aspect of real property from the buying of a council house to the marriage settlement of a ducal estate.

Land is a commodity—but never to be bought or sold like coffee or tea... The Victorians had their sudden surprising vision of what land was capable of producing beyond turnips and the work of serfs; coal, iron, tin—the minerals for industrial expansion—space for railways, for canals, for roadways, and above all for the building of towns. Out of such expectations there had grown the present conurbations in which everyone could have a little home of his own with a garden for flowers and a fence to shut out his neighbours.

If the new councils frowned on old customs like the keeping of pigs, hens and pigeons—and some of them weren't too keen either on man's best friend—at least they now allowed garages and parking places for the new family pets. But humans did not seem to have been created for contentment with their lot. Other aspirations had arisen; a need for space in which to relax, enjoy leisure facilities and indulge in the games and sports deemed necessary to answer the prayer of Juvenal, *'mens sana in corpore sano'*. So far Newtown Development Corporation had not provided much in this line except at the schools, where there were plenty of young healthy bodies though the quality of the minds was yet to be determined. The Corporation planners had up till now been too weighted down by their building schemes to look at the wide open spaces beyond the town, but give them time...

Kemp's knowledge of the Courtenay Trust was vague—any work of this nature which flowed into his office was dealt with by Tony Lambert who enjoyed browsing in the fields of Equity—but he presumed that the land had once been entailed, then brought within the provisions of the Settled Land Acts to keep it—so far as it was possible to do in modern times—in the family. Silas must have been the ideal tenant-for-life; prudent and far-sighted, he had spent only what he had to and invested wisely. With his death it appeared that the trust would come to an end. This meant that Vivian would now be the absolute owner in possession of the whole Courtenay property, in legal parlance: 'the principal mansion, pleasure grounds, park and lands...' and he could do what he damn well liked with it, only subject to the exigencies of the Town and Country Planning Acts. It was not a pleasing prospect.

Where, Kemp wondered, did Venetia stand? By her own demeanour, on pretty favourable ground...

When he reached the Manor the iron gates between the worn stone pillars stood wide open as they had done on the previous night but there was something uninviting about the long drive curving away under the dark foliage of copper beeches which made him hesitate. The little chapel behind the hawthorn hedge on the other side of the road was so bathed in sunshine that even the gravestones round it looked cheerful, so he pushed open the wicket and wandered up the gravel path. In this place the Courtenays had been buried for centuries, along with those of their retainers who had stood by them till death, and any local villagers who had been granted the privilege—presumably through service on the estate.

Silas Courtenay's new grave still had no headstone, and the flowers on it had withered. There had not been many. Rank grass grew high everywhere, and brambles sprawled over the kerbs and low railings of the tombs, the lesser stones half-hidden in a profusion of vegetation. Leaving the path, Kemp surprised a figure bent over with a pair of clippers in her hand as she tried to cut thick stems of ivy from the foot of a gravestone. She straightened up on his approach, a rounded lady with a pleasant face reddened by her exertions. He knew she was a lady as soon as she spoke.

'Lovely morning,' she said, 'but rather warm for this kind of work.' She had a notebook laid on the grass beside her, and a pencil behind her ear. Intrigued, Kemp asked politely what exactly that work was.

'Memorial inscriptions,' she said. 'I'm doing it for the local family history society. Some of these old churchyards are so overgrown that in a few years the stones won't be readable.'

She seemed glad of an excuse to pause for breath, so together they found a seat on a fallen stone where the primitive outline of a skull was almost obscured by creeping moss. Her name, she said, was Lydia Beresford, she was a widow with time on her hands, and had taken a part-time job in the library where she was working on the archives.

'But we haven't got archives in Newtown,' said Kemp, laughing. 'We're not old enough yet...'

'You forget what was here before you came,' said Mrs Beresford tartly, 'and there's plenty of history in the villages if you care to look for it.'

She produced a small trowel from the pocket of her leather jacket and began scratching at the green and yellow lichen on the stone.

'You see, this one died in the Crimea... It even gives his regiment...'

'He's not a Courtenay,' Kemp observed, peering at the incised lettering as she cleared it. 'A subaltern. Boyce, by name...'

'There were Boyces in the Parsonage about that time,' said the lady briskly. 'All gone now, of course, and long forgotten. But if they thought him worth a tombstone it should not go unrecorded.' She was working away gently, prising up the thick clots of moss. 'Look at the rest of it: "A valiant soldier and a worthy man. A loyal friend, mourned by his men." You don't get that kind of tribute in the official records. And people do come, you know, from all over the world to look for the gravestones of their ancestors.'

'Even here? I thought this place was reserved for the Courtenays?'

'Not entirely. It had to serve the village of Ember as well. Not that there's much left of that these days. Dying Ember, I call it...' She was pleased when Kemp laughed. 'Anyway, I don't bother much with the Courtnays—they're well enough documented elsewhere. But, as with other noble families, we do get inquiries from people who like to think they might be related to the main branch, the titled ones. Stuff and nonsense, I say. Mostly Americans, they are. Been to the Mormons who give them a sheaf of papers telling them they're descended from Richard I, or even Charlemagne. Well, we probably all are when you consider the population at the time.'

Kemp was highly amused. It was very agreeable sitting in the sunshine on a tombstone listening to this resourceful lady who had such a keen sense of history but was not taken in by any of its romantic possibilities.

She explained she preferred researching the ordinary families of the villages, the yeoman farmers, the labourers on the land—alas, few of the latter had any headstones at all, though the parish dutifully recorded their passing. 'Far better be descended from an honest workman than a dissolute nobleman,' Mrs Beresford said, with robust good sense. Kemp suspected that, from her accent and authoritative manner, she herself was not exactly lowly-bred but he admired her attitude for its principle.

'Not all Americans come hoping for titled fore-bears,' she conceded. 'There was a young man here recently. Came into the library asking about local paths. Said he was on a walking tour and anxious not to trespass. Now that's something your new folk in Newtown don't give a hoot about. Leaving gates open, and trampling the crops, Mr Kemp, it's no wonder they get themselves disliked.'

'I'm sorry to hear it.' Kemp could find no excuse for what she called 'his folk', apart from disassoci-ating himself from them by saying he always kept to the roads, being an ignorant townsman and terrified of cattle. 'I hope you were able to help this wander-ing American?'

'I advised him to obtain an ordnance survey map from the stationer's which would show him the des-ignated footpaths, but it was something else he mentioned that made me take more interest in him.'

'What was that?'

'He told me he wanted to have a look at Ember because that was his middle name. Of course I had to tell him there wasn't much left of the village, and that it had been owned by the Courtenays for gen-erations. Then it struck me that perhaps he hoped his forebears had come from Ember so I said if he came back the following day I would get out the Parish registers for him and we could go through them to-gether. So many people come, you see, that it's nec-essary to apply to the archivist and make a proper appointment. I did this while the young man waited, and we made a definite date for the following day, the fifteenth of August, but he did not turn up. I was extremely surprised, Mr Kemp, for he had been most polite. I had thought him the best type of quiet American... He had this great haversack—don't they call them backpacks?—which he put down most carefully. Said it contained everything he needed for travelling. It set me thinking of the troubadours of old... Oh, my! Just look at the time!' She got up hurriedly and retrieved her notebook. 'I do so want to finish this little graveyard before lunch. It's been nice talking to you, Mr Kemp, and I hope we may see you in our library one of these days, though I'm afraid we're not very well up in law books,' she finished, archly.

'I'm glad to hear it,' said Kemp. 'Wouldn't want the townsfolk of Newtown to try teaching themselves tort. It's bad enough when they do their own conveyancing!'

He left Mrs Beresford to her voluntary task, and proceeded up the drive towards the Manor. The Dower House was off to the right in a small, not particularly well-tended garden. The rooms too would be small, but the casement windows were pretty and there was a fair-sized paddock fenced off at the rear where horses were grazing. A nice piece of property if put on the open market but, as Arnold Crayshaw had pointed out, it was part of the estate... Kemp had gathered from what Blanche

Courtenay had said last night that she wanted to join Amy Francis in the riding school, but he knew that establishment badly needed capital. Surely, now that the twins had, as the saying went, come into their inheritance, they could not leave their mother out in the cold? She must have been receiving a competence from Silas under the trust as well as the right to reside in the Dower House for her lifetime. But if the trust had come to an end and generosity was at a premium among the younger generation, what then?

I don't know anything about the Courtenay trust, and I don't want to, he said to himself firmly as the drive opened out into its great sweep in front of the mansion. His car was tucked away inconspicuously behind a clump of laurels. There were other cars still strewn about, some twenty of them, presumably belonging to house-guests or to others as yet too lazy to fetch them.

Fumbling for his keys, he was startled by a voice that seemed to come out of the bushes.

'Good morning, Lennox, you're up early.'

He turned and saw Venetia Courtenay standing on the greensward that stretched behind the dark evergreens. She was not alone. Several people, among whom he recognized remnants of last night's party, were strolling on the lawn or sitting on the stone balustrade of the terrace. This side of the house had a pleasanter aspect than the front which looked out, bare-faced, on to the gravelled forecourt and an area of unkempt grassland.

'Come walk with me,' she said, setting off fairly briskly. It was more command than invitation but still difficult to refuse.

'A beautiful garden,' he said, joining her.

'Silas thought so. This is where he sat and counted his money.' She gestured towards the terrace where the last roses were twined along the stonework, enjoying the autumn sun.

Kemp wondered about the old man who had made this south-facing garden, and who had lived over ninety years, thereby thwarting many hopes and aspirations during his lifespan.

'It's a morning for counting one's blessings,' he said.

'How very philosophic!'

They were walking away from the others, which seemed to be her intention.

'Were you often here when your Uncle Silas was alive?'

'Enough to keep up appearances. Mummy insisted, just in case he'd forget we'd ever been born. We lived in a poky little house in Peckham when we weren't away at school. Then Grandma died and Mother was graciously allowed to live in the Dower.' Venetia twisted her lips as she spoke as if they had a bitter taste. Indeed her whole manner was one of petulance and discontent, which sounded strange to Kemp in view of her present supposed good fortune.

'A very boring little man, Uncle Silas,' she went on, 'out of Dickens with a bit of Trollope but not the most riveting character of either...'

'And will you live here now?'

'Heavens, no! I'm not your outdoor type. The place is draughty as hell, and the bedrooms reek of damp. Vivian can pull it down for all I care.'

'It must be a listed building,' Kemp mused, unsure of whether this was the kind of thing she said to everyone, or whether she was putting on an act. Perhaps it was both.

They had reached a seat where a dip in the ground hid them from the house. She sat down, first brushing away damp leaves with her scarf, a red polka-dotted piece of silk which she used negligently like a duster.

'Then they can just unlist it. They'll do exactly what Vivian wants,' she said with complacency. 'Of course he may want to settle down for a while and have house-parties in the grand style... Wasn't it great fun last night?' She'd changed again, sparkling, laughing, her grey eyes dancing. There was more green in them today. 'We could have many more like it. Give dreary old Newtown a bit of a lift...'

'With that amount of champagne you could have it floating. Why did you specifically ask for me to come?' He said it casually but watched for her reaction.

'Because I find the whole idea of crime so fascinating,' she answered promptly, 'and you specialize in crime, don't you, Lennox? But I told you all that. I'd heard about you from Lettice Warrender.'

You were not supposed to doubt the word of a lady but this one gave him no option. Lettice Warrender hadn't seen her for years.

'You wouldn't find crime fascinating if you sat in the Magistrates' Court of a morning,' he said drily. 'That's dreary old Newtown at its nadir.'

'Oh, I'm not interested in petty larceny or incapable drunks. I mean the real stuff. You've been involved in murders, and kidnapping, and finding missing persons, and international spy-rings...' There was no doubt about her excitement; it seemed a pity to throw cold water on it for she was much more attractive when her patrician features had a flush to them and her eyes were warm.

'I'm not James Bond, you know,' he said, 'these things happened to crop up in the course of my work. I'm insatiably curious, that's my trouble.'

'But how do you go about it? That's what I want to know.' She clapped her hands as she had done the night before on seeing the Conga troop. 'I'd love to have been a private detective. Do you think it's too late to start?'

Kemp couldn't help laughing, but for all her ingenuousness there had been a serious edge to her voice, to which he had to respond.

'You wouldn't really like it, Venetia. It's not at all glamorous. Most of it's very dull stuff, sitting around listening to people, making inquiries...'

'Making inquiries, how professional that sounds! How do you begin, this making inquiries?'

'About what?'

'Well, anything. Take a missing person...'

'This is a free country. People can go missing if they've a mind to...' Kemp felt the conversation was getting rather out of hand. He was normally disinclined to talk about himself or his out-of-office activities but she seemed so eager, so genuinely interested, that he found himself growing voluble even on the dull subject of routine inquiries—fresh in his mind in any case.

Venetia Courtenay was a surprisingly good listener.

'And what if the missing person is dead?' she asked when he had stopped.

'Then the body will be found. Bodies always are, unless you can throw them overboard from an ocean liner—and I think there was a chap done for that too...'

'How tremendously exciting it all is!' She unclasped her hands which had been round her knees like a schoolgirl, 'I could go on listening to you for hours, Lennox. But—'she sighed—'it looks as if my guests want me.'

A small group had by now appeared on the edge of the rise, staring vacantly about them like sheep without a leader. Venetia got up but she grasped Kemp's arm. 'I shall see you again soon, I hope,' she said breathlessly. 'You really must call on us.'

'You mean when you are in residence with your brother?' She was playing lady of the manor again. 'I thought you said you couldn't abide life in the country? Sydney Smith had no relish for it either . . . Called it a kind of healthy grave.'

'Actually—' Venetia flipped her scarf at a falling leaf— 'actually, I haven't yet made up my mind. Proby and I have our London flat, of course, but there's not much fun there with Proby working all hours in the market . . .' Her pinstriped husband might have been a porter at Billingsgate. 'Don't you think all this making of money is the most frightful bore?'

'You would prefer it to burst about your head in a shower of gold as happened to Danaë?'

'What a way with words you lawyers have!' She was mocking him but there was subtle flattery too, the kind that on this Sunday morning and in this setting was beginning to make him lightheaded. The conversation continued in this manner as they sauntered slowly up the lawn, for Venetia seemed in no hurry to join her guests.

When he finally relinquished her to them and was driving back to Newtown he still had the uneasy feeling that he had been, for a short time, hypnotized. People who talk too much generally do so out of self-importance, yet that was just what he had been doing with Venetia Courtenay. He wondered if he had been trying to impress her...

In his nondescript flat which was both home and bolthole, he regarded its folkweave curtains and commonplace furniture with disfavour. He crossed to the window and gazed down at the cement-mixer in the builder's yard below. Why haven't I got a garden with lawns and rose-bushes, he asked himself? I can well afford to...

He got himself a drink and shook the glossy supplements out of the Sunday papers, but even this trivial exercise only seemed to increase his mood of discontent. We're back in the eighteenth century, he thought morosely, gawping at expensive high fashion in the gardens and courtyards of great houses, we hanker after the lifestyles of the aristocracy and long to tread their marble halls. I behaved like any feudal serf today in the presence of Venetia Courtenay.

Despite his solitary habits, he had become an excellent cook—mainly through trial and error—and a good lunch restored his sense of humour. At least my food's better than theirs if last night's 'do' is anything to go by. And they certainly have some deplorable mannerisms, he thought as he washed his dishes in the small, cramped kitchen.

He couldn't help smiling when he thought of the way Venetia referred to her husband as Proby...Kemp's daily help, Mrs Blackwell, always called her spouse by his surname. 'Blackwell's proper

poorly,' she would say, or: 'Me and Blackwell, we're
off to the whist-drive.'

Could this be a case of the workers aping their
betters, or was it the other way round? But in Mrs
Blackwell's speech it meant no disparagement, rather
it gave her husband his place and his dignity. From
the mouths of the Courtenays, both mother and
daughter, it sounded like casual contempt—the kind
of passing reference an eighteenth-century squire
might make to his gamekeeper. Whatever it was,
Lewis Proby obviously didn't count for much in their
estimation. Presumably Venetia had married him
during the lean years when old Silas had gone on
living contrary to all expectations. If Proby had just
been a meal-ticket he might well have outlived his
usefulness and been reduced as a consequence to his
present single name status on par with a pet dog or
one of Blanche's gee-gees.

Reflecting on names, Kemp was reminded of
Venetia's outrage when he had passed on to her his
flippant thoughts about the coat-of-arms so splen-
didly emblazoned on the ceiling at the Manor. She
had rounded on him, all guns firing, and declared it
was the Tudors who were the upstarts, scarce a cup-
ful of royal blood to their name, whereas the Courtenays were of more ancient lineage. He had been
amused at her vehemence, seeing such pride as out-
of-date, and even faintly risible. Did it really matter
in this day and age? In the North the saying went:
'Clogs to clogs in three generations.' How long did

it take for even the bluest of blood to run thin, leaving any nobility they ever had only in the name?

Now that he was back in his own mundane familiar surroundings Kemp began to put things into proper perspective. This high-born lady, this Venetia Courtenay, he decided, she was up to something, she was playing some game... She had inveigled Lettice into bringing him to the Manor, she had deliberately sought him out, and today she had engaged him in light conversation which yet held some serious point—if only he knew what it was. As she herself had swung from mood to mood, so she had carried him. He disliked the feeling; she made him nervous. He hoped he would never have to see her again.

FOUR

THAT HOPE was fulfilled—at least for the time being. Lennox Kemp heard nothing from the Courtenays for the next few weeks, nor did he give them much thought as he busied himself with the work for which he was paid, some particularly difficult civil litigation both onerous and time-consuming.

It was for this reason also that he was unable to pursue as diligently as he might otherwise have done the missing husband of Julie Sorrento. He did what he could from his office desk, handed over the thin file to his new articled clerk, Frank Fosdyke, and sent him off to interview Lucky Luciano's workmates.

Frank was an eager young man, not as brash as the previous one with the initialled briefcase but just as anxious to make his way in his chosen calling. He was glad to exchange annotating statutory instruments for a morning out in the tomato houses, now being steam-heated and fumigated at the end of the growing season. He provided himself with an Italian phrase-book, and hoped for revelations.

He returned disappointed.

'They all knew Lucky Sorrento,' he reported, 'but he seems to have been a taciturn sort of chap, never

speaking much to anyone. Lucky he was not—at
least in their opinion—not with the sort of wife he'd
married who couldn't even cook spaghetti and never
took the kids to Mass.'

'Did they know about this lottery prize?'

'One of them—' Frank looked at his notes '—Mr
Fabriani, said he'd met the brother who came over.
The prize money wasn't much and they'd spent it all
on that holiday.'

'So there wasn't any reason for Luciano to go back
to Sicily for the rest of it?'

'Apparently not. But Mr Fabriani and the others
did say that Mr Sorrento was a bit of a misery. He
was always going on about the allotment he lost last
spring. I looked into that. It was one of those plots
the Council took back when they wanted to develop
the land for housing. The allotment-holders got
compensation but poor old Lucky hadn't had his for
long so he didn't get much. Seems to have rankled
with him. He'd go up there after work and just sit
watching the bulldozers. That's where that photograph was taken, by the way. I recognized the fence
at the back.' Frank was rather pleased with himself
for this piece of observation. 'What's our next step?'

'Well, there's not a lot we can do. We can't issue a
summons for maintenance when we don't know
where he is. We'll just have to wait until he turns up
somewhere. In the meantime, you trot round to that
address on the caravan site and see if Mrs Sorrento
has had any news of him. Perhaps she'll succumb to

your youthful charm and tell you more than she did me.'

Frank didn't get the chance to try.

'Place was all locked up,' he said. 'I did speak to a neighbour. She didn't know anything about the Sorrentos and obviously didn't want to, but she'd heard that Mrs Sorrento had taken the children and gone back to her mother in London. Somewhere in Camden Town, she thought.'

'Well, she's off our hands, then. I bet the local Social Services will be pleased. You might just check with them, Frank. A phone call will do.'

Later, Frank came back, grinning broadly. 'You were right. Mrs Sorrento had a week's money from them just after she came to you, and they've not seen her since. They wish Camden Town the best of British... Well, not in so many words,' he added hastily, remembering that Kemp was a stickler for accuracy.

But Kemp was off on another tack. 'We still send our beggars from parish to parish, hoping someone will take them off our hands. Times don't change.' He was following his own line of thought.

So was Frank.

'Funny, though, a chap like Luciano Sorrento doing a bunk like that. Most of the Italians I spoke to are family men themselves. They didn't think he'd go off and leave his kids. His wife, perhaps, but not his children ...'

'Perhaps he knew his wife had a mother to go to. She never told me that. She never told me very much, come to think of it.' Kemp was conscious now of how very unsatisfactory his interview with Julie Sorrento had been. Her scruffy, slatternly looks and manner of speech, the incident of the child and the ink bottle—hilarious though it was in retrospect—these things had caused him to make too quick an assessment, too lazy a judgement; he had accepted too easily the appearance without searching for the reality.

'You know, Frank,' he said, 'I quite forgot to ask if her husband's passport was missing. Damn it...'

Frank Fosdyke was encouraged by the admission. If his principal could make mistakes there was hope that similar omissions on his own part in the future might be pardonable.

'They both must have had passports,' he said promptly, 'they'd been to Italy on holiday once—so Mr Fabriani told me. Mrs Sorrento hated it. Said his family over there lived like pigs.'

'That would hardly have endeared her to the Sicilians... My God, she even mentioned the Mafia! I wonder if she was having me on? Anyway, we've done all we can, explored every avenue, left no stone unturned, etcetera, and still we haven't found him.' Kemp sighed. 'Ah, well, life is full of loose ends, it was never meant to be tidy...' On that philosophical note the Sorrento file was returned to its meagre space in the filing cabinet.

That had been almost a month ago and other things had by then intervened to absorb Kemp's attention, including his excursion into the very different world of the Courtenays. From time to time Frank, like the good pupil he was, would bring the file forward and they would both gaze at its grey cover with glum dissatisfaction.

'Send in that Legal Aid form,' Kemp said eventually. 'I don't suppose anything else is going to turn up in the matter...'

What did turn up was in fact a body, and that Kemp only heard about quite inadvertently.

He was talking to Sergeant Cobbins in the lobby of the Newtown Magistrates' Court one morning. They had had the doubtful pleasure of sharing a client at the early session, a lively lad who had taken and driven away someone else's car in order to impress his girlfriend. Kemp had managed to get him off lightly but the Sergeant bore no ill-will.

'He'll do it again, mark my words, Mr Kemp. He's a wrong 'un and he'll go for the wheels every time. By the way, that Luciano Sorrento you asked about a while back...'

'What about him?'

'You hadn't heard? They found his body. The station should have let you know at the time but you only making a routine inquiry, like, they never thought... I was busy on leave myself, otherwise I'd have given you a buzz.'

'When? Where? Come on, Harry!'

'No mystery about it,' Detective-Sergeant Cobbins said somewhat huffily. 'Body found in the claypit up Burrow Hill. Body identified by sorrowing widow. Inquest verdict death by misadventure. Could've been suicide, of course, but who wants to distress the bereaved?'

'When did all this happen?'

Cobbins rubbed his chin with a large hand. 'Let's see now. Chap with dog found him—be around two weeks back. Been dead a while, though. Cause of death, broken skull, multiple injuries—he'd fallen quite a ways. No trouble about identifying him, he'd his working clothes on, pay-slip in his pocket—aye, and his wages too, so he'd not been robbed. Left a widow and two kids...'

'I know all about his family. Hell's bells, I've been sitting on that file for weeks!'

'Well, don't blame me, Mr Kemp. As I said, I wasn't around at the time. Only got back yesterday. Anyway, it was all cut and dried. His employers, Everetts, they sent a witness to the inquest to say he'd gone missing from work, and that was confirmed by the widow...'

'You mean he's dead and buried? Wasn't there anything in the paper?'

'Didn't merit much, did it? Italian worker falls in claypit after a drinking bout. What did you want, banner headlines? It was in the local, small para. What's it to you, Mr Kemp?'

Kemp was resigned to the fact that at times of extreme busyness his reading of the local press was often confined to items of professional interest only, such as neighbourhood protests about planning, notices of impending street works, licensing applications, and the entertaining accounts of the numerous on-going battles within the Council Chambers.

The Sergeant's revelation had shaken him. He was disposed to find a scapegoat for his irritation.

'Why the hell didn't she let me know?'

'Who?'

'The grieving widow you talked of. Mrs. Sorrento. She was the one who came to me first about her missing husband.'

'I don't know, do I? I never met the lady. Inspector Upshire was the one who saw her.' Sergeant Cobbins was sounding huffy again, and Kemp could appreciate his feelings.

'Sorry, Harry, didn't mean to take it out on you. It's my own fault. I should have been keeping a more careful watch on local affairs. I'll have a word with the Inspector.'

'Won't be easy, Mr Kemp, he's got a lot on his plate at the moment.'

Kemp ignored that; everybody was too busy these days. But John Upshire and he were good friends quite apart from the common ground of their respective duties, and a phone call that evening inviting the Inspector out for a drink had them both in the bar of the Cabbage White by nine o'clock.

They were easy in each other's company, aware of a mutual need. Since the death of his wife, John Upshire also lived alone and the nature of his position in the community tended to restrict his social contacts even had he been a clubbable man—which he was not. He had reluctant admiration for Kemp's stubborn belief in some abstract concept of justice, while deprecating the unorthodox methods he sometimes used in pursuit of it. Upshire would not have put it in these words though Kemp might well have done. He, in his turn, respected Upshire's intelligence and his staunch adherence to Police regulations—but he would twist the Inspector's arm if their interests ever clashed.

Tonight they talked of more humdrum matters, the incidence of local vandalism and suburban burglary, and the tendency of the Newtown young to indulge in mindless villainy.

'I blame the schools,' said Upshire moodily, 'all that free-wheeling stuff...'

'Why not the parents,' said Kemp, not altogether seriously, 'if you must blame somebody? Most of them have come out from London's East End, and there weren't many angels among them when you did your stint in the Met.'

'Then it's high time they mended their ways. They've been given decent housing, decent wages and a jolly good standard of living.'

'So has everyone else. It's all relative, you know. They just see bigger houses, flashier cars. Going up in the world doesn't necessarily straighten out a criminal bent—though it might make them smarter in all senses of the word.'

The two men shifted the small coin of their daily occupations around for a while before Kemp came to the point.

'This Italian worker, Sorrento, who died recently—didn't you know I was looking for him?'

'H'm. No, I did not. You'd only spoken casually to Sergeant Cobbins, and he was away when Sorrento's body was found. Why? Would it have made any difference?'

'I suppose not. Depends when he died.'

'The pathologist couldn't be certain. He'd been dead about three weeks before that dog started rooting around in the undergrowth at the bottom of the pit. That would be about the middle of September, and you'll remember we'd had that heavy rain at the end of August. Made the clay slippery and dangerous. He'd bashed his head on a rock when he fell and according to the path report death would have been instantaneous. Just as well for the poor bloke. It's a pretty deserted spot out there, nobody would have heard him if he'd cried out.'

'No suggestion of foul play?'

'You mean, did someone chuck him over? It's not beyond the bounds of possibility, but from our investigations, highly unlikely. He'd consumed a lot of alcohol, he'd rubber-soled shoes on and there were marks at the top of the pit where he could have slid.

You knew he'd had one of these allotments up there?'

'So I've heard.'

'Well, one of his mates said he'd still go to the hut he used to have—the developers hadn't quite reached it—and sit there lamenting his loss and consoling himself with vino. We found plenty of empty wine bottles scattered about. He must have been really pissed that night...'

'He staggered out, missed his footing and slid to his death?'

'That's the theory. Of course he might have been past caring. I understand he was depressed about losing his plot on those allotments. Can't blame him for that. I'm a gardening man myself and I can guess what it must have meant to him having a bit of ground to grow things on. It could have been suicide, but you know Mr McKenna, the coroner, he'll go for misadventure every time—particularly when there's a widow.'

'The widow, yes... You met her?'

'Julie Sorrento, but not as Italian as her name. Pure Cockney, I'd say, feckless and not overbright but what can you expect these days?' Upshire seemed about to return to the evils of modern education so Kemp steered him gently back.

'How did she take it?'

'Surprisingly well, I thought. We knew who he was right away from the stuff in his pockets. I sent one of my better types to the address at The Willows to

break the news. I accompanied her to the morgue
myself. Nasty, that... But she was all right. Shed a
few tears. I would have left a WPC with her that
night but Mrs Sorrento said she'd be OK, she'd go to
her mother's till the inquest. She wasn't bad in court,
either. A bit weepy, but not more than you'd expect
in the circumstances. McKenna took her through it
gently. She told him her husband had been upset over
the allotment business, he'd taken to drinking
heavily, and he'd been coming in at all hours with his
feet soaking from wandering about up on the site.
Sometimes he'd get so drunk he'd not come in at all
and spend the night sleeping it off at the house of one
of his mates, so she wasn't unduly worried at first.
But when he didn't come back after the weekend, she
phoned Everetts. She didn't fancy going to the police—said her husband wouldn't have wanted it because back in Sicily the police chief would like as not
be in with the Mafia...' The Inspector chuckled. 'I
nearly told her I wouldn't mind his pay cheque.
Anyway, she just thought she'd been deserted. She
might be a bit dumb but like all wives these days she
knows her matrimonial rights, so she went along to
the DHSS.'

'Who referred her to me,' said Kemp glumly. 'End
of story.'

'That's about it, Lennox. Another pint? We're
both walking home.'

Kemp studied the stained beer mats. He was in a
low mood, and cross with himself. He did not often

fail people, and he felt he had failed Julie Sorrento. He expressed something of this to the Inspector when he came back and put down the two glasses.

'Nothing you could have done, old man. Luciano Sorrento might well have been dead by the time she went to see you.'

'Yes, but...' Kemp felt he had to have a grumble at someone. 'Why on earth didn't she let me know when he'd been found?'

'Aw, come on, Lennox. What did you want, a courtesy call? The woman had quite enough to contend with, her husband killed in an accident, she's got kids to look after, then there's the inquest, and on top of that she's got to get him properly buried—though the local priest was a great help over that, I understand. What's got into you? You're not usually so hard on the underprivileged. I didn't think much of Mrs Sorrento myself—one of life's inadequates, I'd say—and I can't imagine she ever thought of you as her lawyer.'

'You're probably right.' Kemp sighed. 'She treated me as just another branch of the welfare state, the one that's supposed to chase missing husbands for maintenance.'

'Well, you can't get maintenance from a corpse.' John Upshire took the practical view. 'She didn't do too badly. Everetts were generous, and Luciano's workmates had a whipround. She'd enough for the fare.'

'The fare? Where?' Kemp knew it sounded idiotic.

'To fly her and the kids to Sicily. It was what his family wanted when they heard of the tragedy. She'd a call from the brother, said he couldn't afford to come over for the funeral but they all wanted to look after her and the children.'

'I know all about the brother,' said Kemp, testily. 'How very family-minded these Sicilians are! Must be the effect of the Mafia.'

Upshire glared. 'Now, don't you start. There's been quite enough jokes on that topic down at the station. Which reminds me, the Burgess boys come up for sentencing next week. Now there's a pair who'd be no use to any Mafia. They've bungled every job they've ever been on...'

'Thanks to good police work,' said Kemp tactfully as he downed his drink.

'That's what I like about crime in these parts—' the Inspector was relaxed, and inclined to be jocular, a side of him rarely revealed to his subordinates—'it's so disorganized you can pick them off like pigeons. Most of these local louts haven't got a brain between them!'

'Must be something to do with the standard of education,' said Kemp innocently.

FIVE

ALTHOUGH LENNOX KEMP had a ticket for the Newtown Public Library he rarely used it. Over the years he tended to buy rather than borrow the books he wanted to read, mainly because they were the kind he could read again—though he never did. Although his interests ran more to biography, history, literary memoirs and philosophy (of the lighter sort), even the novels he carefully chose he would put down at the end with a sense of the pleasure he would get on re-reading them at some future date, as if he were storing up rations against rainy times.

Having been reminded, however, by meeting Mrs Beresford that even brash modern Newtown possessed some source of culture, he went into the library one day, undeterred by its outward appearance, depressing purple brick with a grey slate roof. Only some fancy embellishment of fretted dark wood in the Swiss chalet or cuckoo-clock style distinguished it from the Police Station further up the road and the public toilets on the corner. All three buildings had been designed by the same architect, possibly after a heavy lunch.

The interior was surprisingly comfortable but there were few people about. Kemp found a new biography of Henry VIII, recently recommended, and was on his way out when he caught sight of Lydia Beresford at a table by the window.

She smiled a welcome so he went over to her.

'Do sit down, Mr Kemp. I'm very glad to see you again. I enjoyed our chat the last time we met.'

'You seem to be busy.' The table was covered with parish registers and charts.

'Actually, I'm off duty. This is my private work on family histories. That's supposed to be very good...' She nodded at the book in his hand.

'So I gather. Not so much bluff King Hal as a lesson in how to run a totalitarian state.'

'He was a monster,' she said decidedly. 'He quite literally put the fear of God into all his subjects, Catholic and Protestant alike... You will be the one to appreciate his spy network!'

Kemp raised his eyebrows.

'Oh, I've been hearing about you, Mr Kemp.'

He shook his head. 'Much exaggerated, I'm sure. Did your young American ever come back to the library?'

'No, he didn't. I'm very disappointed in him. It was a discourtesy not to return as he promised. And yet, at the time, he seemed so genuinely interested, and he was such a very polite young man. I cannot understand it.'

'Perhaps he was disheartened when he saw how little there was left of Ember.'

'He did say he might go and have a look at it.' But Mrs Beresford was not inclined to give up her small grievance lightly. 'I asked him how he got the name, and of course he didn't know. He just said he'd been told it was English. None of the rest of the family had it, and there were a lot of them running a restaurant in New York. I took some trouble to go through the registers myself but there were no surnames of Ember in the records—I hadn't expected there would be. People in this part of the country didn't get their names from villages... That's not the point, Mr Kemp. He should have had the courtesy to telephone if he couldn't keep his appointment.'

She ruffled through the papers on her table. 'Now, where did I put that slip I made out for him? I might as well cancel it. Ah, here it is.'

'May I?'

Kemp glanced at the form requesting the baptismal and burial registers for the parish of Ember, clearly written in Mrs Beresford's neat hand.

'Was that his name?'

'Carlos E. Rossi. Yes, he spelled it for me. I thought it sounded Italian, but then he was from New York and I have found that many Americans do have names which sound foreign to us. Anyway, it was only his middle name I was interested in.'

'Did he tell you anything else about himself?'

'He said he was working his way through college, this was his first trip abroad and he was doing it on the cheap.'

'He was a student?'

Mrs Beresford considered. 'Well, I should say a mature student. He'd be in his thirties—that's young to me. He was rather nice-looking, dark hair, and that smooth olive skin you see a lot of in New York.'

'You're very perceptive, Mrs Beresford.'

She bridled at the compliment. 'I had time on my hands that day he came in, and I found him quite charming... But there you are,' she went on briskly, 'he didn't bother to come back. Probably found something more exciting to do than rummage in dusty old records. I do tend to get carried away by my hobby.'

As Kemp left the library he reflected that Lydia Beresford was possibly lonely, well-provided for in everything except companionship. Had she not had this interest in other people's histories she might have found her niche organizing charities—the modern equivalent of taking soup to the poor. She had felt slighted that the charming young American had not returned to share in what, to her, would have been a pleasurable excursion into known territory, whereas he had been on a walking tour, and had simply walked on and out of her life.

Kemp was far more intrigued by her remark about himself. Now, who had she been talking to? His mind leapt to the Courtenays and he realized that, subconsciously, they had never been far from his thoughts; even to the extent that they might have influenced his choice of reading. Lydia Beresford would be of an age with Blanche and they might well move in the same circle. It was odd, he reflected, how one classified people by their accent and demeanour, hazarded a guess at their social milieu and then, having put them into some vague category, felt free to ask if they knew so-and-so. When next he met Mrs Beresford he would find out if he was right.

In the meantime as he walked back to his office the same pattern of ideas remained with him.

By its very nature, Newtown lacked an upper structure in its society. There was a thick substratum of workers, skilled and unskilled, blue-collared and white, a solid layer of tradesmen and owners of small businesses, a sprinkling of semi professionals, and a top-dressing of medical men, lawyers and clergy. One had to look outside the town itself to find any relics of what used to be called 'gentlefolk'. Even at Castleton where the Warrenders were holding on by the skin of their teeth, the Reverend Clive Cavendish, whose family, according to Lettice, stretched back to the Conquest, had joined his ancestors and the present incumbent at St James's Rectory was a jazzy young Londoner who was doing his best to get his congregation swinging with him.

Kemp moved through this newly-sprung town which he both loved and despaired of, past the windows of estate agents and building societies, the ironmongers and the greengrocers, under the giant portals of the supermarket (designed in the Greek mode but stumped for space) and into the central square. The sapling trees were actually growing—not by any means the first, but the Council could be stubborn—and the pseudo-mediaeval cobblestones were smoother now than in the early days when they tried tempers and footwear alike.

He climbed the stairs to his office, and was way-laid by Elvira.

'Can you squeeze in a late appointment? A Mr Courtenay—something to do with planning. I said five-thirty...'

'That's all right. Bring the mail in early, and I'll see him afterwards. Has Mrs Francis arrived?'

'She's waiting for you, Mr Kemp.'

Amy was always early, as if anxious to get any business over as soon as possible. Today she had brought him instructions for a partnership agreement.

'Of course it's only tentative at the moment but I wanted my suggestions down on paper so that I could show them to Blanche Courtenay.'

'She's decided to go in with you, then?'

Amy turned up her eyes in mock helplessness. Indecision on the part of anyone, even herself, was an irritant, although she had endless patience with horses and small children.

'Hopefully—as people keep saying on television. Of course she's always said how much she wants to... But this time it might just come off. She says she's only waiting for the actual money to come through.'

'How much is she bringing in?'

'Fifty thou.' Amy saw his eyes widen. 'It's what she herself suggested. I'm not a fool, Lennox, I'll only believe it when I see it. Blanche Courtenay is notoriously unreliable. I suppose it was all those years of uncertainty... And don't say it's a bad basis for a partnership. I know Blanche. I can handle her. I'm very fond of her as a matter of fact.'

'And you need the cash to expand the school?'

'That's about it.'

'Presumably the money is coming to her from the closure of the Trust?'

'In return for giving up her right to live in the Dower, yes. And she's to have one of the cottages at Ember. At least that'll free her from the terrible twins.'

'Tut-tut, Amy, they're her children.'

'And doesn't Blanche know it? They've been nothing but a pack of trouble, those two, since the moment they were born.'

Kemp looked at the notes she had given him. 'It looks a sensible proposition to me—so long as the money is forthcoming.'

'You could have a word with Mr Crayshaw. Might get things moving a bit.' Amy didn't believe in holding her horses if she could see a gap in the hedge.

Kemp laughed. 'It'll have to be a very discreet word. You know what trustees are like, they hold their cards close to their chests.'

'I'm sure you'll find a way.'

'Well, that's what you pay me for. You said Mrs Courtenay has wanted to join up with you for some time. Why didn't she ask Silas for the money? He could well afford to help her.'

'Because to him the Trust was sacred. I think he was more generous to Blanche than she makes out. I mean, he'd never let her starve, far from it, but on capital moneys he was adamant. I met the old boy a few times, and rather liked him. Had all his wits about him—even at ninety. Clever as a fox. He was no country squire, he took nothing out of the estate for himself.'

'So I understand.' Kemp had been doing his own research. Amy Francis was his client, and if she was acquiring funds it was his business to make sure the source was dependable. 'Silas made his money in that timber firm he had on the Thames. He didn't retire from that until he was over seventy, and he got a fortune out of it when it was sold to one of the multinationals.'

Amy sniffed. 'The Courtenays never, never speak of where Uncle Silas got all his wealth. That was trade, you know. Not nice.'

'But a riding school's different, eh?'

'You and I know it's not. It's a business like any other. But give Blanche her due, she's got an eye for a good pony. She'd have done better breeding horses than children ... Quite apart from the money, I'll be getting someone who'll be useful to me as a guide when I come to replenish my stock. And, don't forget, she has the kind of social contacts my establishment needs.'

Amy was shrewd. She had given the matter a lot of thought.

'Talking of social contacts, do you know a Mrs Beresford?'

'Lydia Beresford? She's an old friend of Blanche's. Her husband was the medical superintendent at the hospital years ago. He'd dead now, I believe. I don't know her very well myself. I'm not quite of that generation, no matter what you think.'

Kemp gallantly indicated that he had thought no such thing, and described how he had met Mrs Beresford and that she must have been talking to someone about him.

Amy nodded. 'That would be Blanche,' she said. 'Lydia Beresford's probably the only person she's at all intimate with in Newtown these days. Of course Lydia was a Cavendish before she married . . .'

'And therefore eligible for inclusion in the charmed circle. There can't be many of them left.'

Amy caught the note of sarcasm. 'You're very quick on our little social snobberies, aren't you? Believe me, my establishment couldn't survive without all the dear little girls whose Papas have aspirations—often beyond their means.'

'Then it's high time I got on with preparing this agreement. I'll let you have a draft along the lines you've suggested, and we can fill in the details later.'

Amy got to her feet, but at the door she turned and remarked, casually: 'I suppose you've heard the rumours about what the Lord Vivian is going to do with the Manor?'

'Lord Vivian? Has he been ennobled?'

'It's what they're calling him—and only partly in fun. The Lord Vivian and his Lady.' Amy gave one of her characteristic snorts.

'You mean Venetia?'

'Who else? Those two act as one—and not at all properly either.'

'Gossip, Amy? That's not like you.'

'I'd call a spade a spade if the word wasn't so unmentionable. But have you heard the other rumours?'

'I close my ears. Reason flies out of the window when rumour comes in.' In view of his later appointment Kemp was not going to be drawn.

'There's talk of a caravan park, camping grounds and even a venue for pop festivals.' Her brilliant blue eyes were alight with indignation.

'I doubt if the County planners will go along with any of that.'

'Go along with it? They'll swallow it hook, line and sinker if it's going to bring in money!'

'You take a jaundiced view of our protectors of the countryside. They are there to guard our imperishable heritage.' Kemp didn't believe a word of such anodyne phrases.

Neither, apparently, did Amy Francis.

'And everyone in my riding classes will be picked for the British team at the next Olympics!'

With this parting shot she closed the door firmly behind her.

She was not the only one that day with sights trained on the County planners. Vivian Courtenay not only took aim, he fired with gusto.

'Pretty dim lot, these bods out at County Hall,' he drawled, 'they're strangled in red tape. Can't speak a word of decent English, their mouths are so stuffed with paper!'

The interview was not going well. If Courtenay had come for advice, Kemp wondered why he had bothered. Vivian had, as he put it, boned up on the subject and knew it all, so that he treated Kemp's patient explication of basic planning law as so much legal jargon, required hearing for lesser breeds but to a man of his standing a lot of hokum. Vivian used such words often, in short bursts like the splutter of a popgun. He had draped himself over his chair, his legs stretched out elegantly along the carpet while, half-turned towards Kemp, he opened his mind to the lawyer on the benefits his schemes would bring to Newtown.

'Can't make these idiotic officials see it my way,' he complained, 'but I've got the ear of one or two Councillors—old Frobisher for one, Ferdy Frobisher was at Rugby with me.' Vivian laid a delicately white finger on the side of his aristocratic nose in a gesture which, in a lesser breed, would have been vulgar. 'Wheels within wheels, that's how it goes, eh, Kemp?'

Kemp pushed a folder across the desk. 'But to get any wheels started,' he said placidly, 'there are a number of forms to be filled in. Take them. You will find them most surprisingly lucid.'

Vivian Courtenay glanced at the folder with distaste before merely sliding it towards him and placing his elbow upon it as he waved a languid arm in dismissal of its contents.

'I've an architect chappie does all that tiresome stuff. I'm an ideas man, myself...' Kemp had no doubt of it; it was the quality of the ideas whirling around inside the head of this greenery-yallery, not quite Grosvenor Gallery young man that was worrying. Kemp couldn't make up his mind whether Vivian was all that he seemed. To take him at face value, he was so wildly dislikeable, such a posturing puppydog, so bereft of the proper instincts which should have been concomitant with his breeding and education, he could have been acting out a parody of the part. Yet behind the *enfant terrible* façade Kemp glimpsed a subtle intelligence, caught now and then the flicker of another personality, and one not altogether at ease. There was an odd shifting of the eyes, there were sudden jumpy movements, evidence of a lack of synchronization between the levels of speech and thought.

So while Vivian talked of how he would out-Woburn Woburn and bring more money into Newtown than Peter de Savary had to Cornwall, Kemp watched other signals, listened for soundings from deeper waters, tried to get a fuller picture of this scion of the Courtenays, this twin to Venetia.

'We would want you to form a company for us, of course,' Vivian was saying. 'Proby's idea. V. & V. Enterprises. Good, eh?'

'Terrific.'

'Proby says it's all the rage nowadays. Tax liabilities and all that.' Again the airy flourish of the hand as if such matters were no longer his concern, he having already mastered their implications.

'I gather that your sister will be a director along with yourself, then?'

Again restlessness came to the surface. Courtenay sprang lightly to his feet and began pacing the room, not without a certain willowy grace. He'd be better as a ballet dancer than a business tycoon, Kemp thought irrelevantly, perhaps an artistic temperament has been thrown in with the other spurious attributes.

'Of course Venetia's in on this. She's the one with the bright ideas ... Not that I'm without them,' Vivian added hastily, 'but it's when we put our heads together that we're inspirational.' He clasped his hands at the back of his neck as he turned and looked down on Kemp from his considerable height like a stork contemplating a frog. 'What do you think of our plans to date, Kemp? Ain't they something?'

It was difficult to get used to these sudden transitions in tone, one minute the bray of the know-all braggart, the next the uncertain attempt at a kind of matey slang as if to find the common touch, almost a childlike appeal for approval. Kemp suddenly remembered that young Courtenay had never known a father...

'They are...interesting.' It wasn't for Kemp to say yea or nay; it would be up to the County planners, and he stressed the fact.

Vivian threw his elegant arms about before folding himself into his chair again. 'We'll have to organize a lobby. Isn't that the way it's done? Get some of the local bigwigs to see the potential...'

'They're a bit thin on the ground hereabouts,' Kemp pointed out with a smile. Where had Courtenay been all these years if he hadn't noticed? He put it to him.

'Of course I'm not familiar with your new town. Wasn't around when it was growing up, was I? Travelled, you know. The Grand Tour they used to call it.' A sneer had come into his voice. 'Not that Venetia and I could do that in any style, thanks to old Money-Guts here at the Manor. Gave us a pittance, that's what he did.'

'You're speaking of the Trust?'

'I bloody am. How Silas wangled it I don't know, but there he was, allowed to squat like a toad, dribbling out the money in pennies. Told us over and over again how he was paying our school fees but

there was never enough pocket money, so that I for
one had to exist like those oiks on scholarships! And
then he cut my allowance because I wouldn't try for
some damn red-brick university...'

It appeared—not very surprisingly—that Vivian
had failed to get into either Oxford or Cambridge,
and any lesser institution was unthinkable. There was
real resentment here, and a bitterness which had en-
dured.

'Your uncle was preserving the estate,' Kemp observed mildly, 'under the provisions of the Trust.'

'Which he bloody well set up! Oh, old Silas knew
what he was doing, all right. Keeping us out of our
inheritance for as long as he could. He'd have been
glad if we'd never been born. Well, it's all mine now,
and I hope he rots in hell.'

The venom in Courtenay's voice made Kemp sit
up. This was more than youthful spite; there was
underlying violence dangerously close to the surface. He recalled Venetia's discontented petulance
when she too had spoken of her uncle. Had these two
been irreversibly warped by their years of waiting in
the wings, by the prize dangled before their eyes but
out of reach, expectations unrealized, hope de-
ferred—perhaps for too long? In her it had seemed
mere pettiness, the pouting peevishness of a spoilt
woman yet, to Kemp she had also shown those
abrupt changes of mood which he now saw mir-
rored in her brother. The physical resemblance between the twins Kemp had taken for granted, as he

had the similarity of some of their mannerisms, but to be confronted by this burning inner rancour shared by both was like standing too close to a brushwood fire. These were startling thoughts, and had to be quickly reined in.

'You've indicated that the company I am to form will be run by you and your sister. On an equal basis?'

'Naturally.'

'Now, as to the capital. You, of course, are the owner of the estate, Mr Courtenay. I'm afraid I don't know what Mrs Proby's position is, financially...'

'You don't need to know that.' The grey eyes, so like hers but lacking the luminous quality, flicked to the side. 'I'm looking after Venetia's interests. Anyway, there'll be a bit for her from the Trust. What's it they call it?'

'A portion? A moiety?'

'Some legal rigmarole...'

Vivian seemed anxious to leave that avenue unexplored. When Kemp—admittedly more out of a personal curiosity than from any requirement for the company forms he must complete—pursued it, Vivian shied off, drumming his long fingers on the desktop impatiently. He seemed to know less, or pretended to know less, of his sister's affairs than he did about planning regulations or company formation—and in both these areas his knowledge was on a high point of ignorance.

'You'll get on with our business, then, Kemp?' Vivian, rising to his feet eventually, was once more the lord of the manor. 'I'll give these to Caldecott.' He picked up the folder and tucked it under his arm. 'Have a dekko at my plans, won't you? Try and persuade these dunderheads on the planning committee to see things my way...'

Kemp knew better than to make any such promise. He opened the door politely as Vivian Courtenay swept through, and decided that easy courtesy was the last he'd show him. Then he returned to his desk to riffle glumly through the copies Vivian had brought with him, the lists of projects, the half-drawn sketches and diagrams, a hotch-potch of fancy schemes and unlikely ventures.

He sat back and thought carefully over his interview with Courtenay. It was a habit of his to do so if there had been puzzling aspects so that, when fresh in the mind, things registered which might otherwise remain undetected.

The man's reluctance to speak of his sister, his nervousness when her name was mentioned... Kemp wondered if Vivian was actually afraid of her. It made a kind of sense. For all their likeness to one another, Venetia was the cleverer of the two in Kemp's estimation, and, despite the masculine element of latent violence in the brother, she might well be the stronger character—for good or evil.

The twins had shared a poisonous draught in their growing years, the bitter taste was still on their lips; how deep was it in their hearts?

SIX

KEMP WAS PLEASED to have a telephone call from
Archie Gillorn's wife, Florence. No, he was not doing anything at the weekend. Yes, he'd be delighted
to visit them. It had been a long time, but pressure of
work, you know... How was Archie? Only the ar-
thritis? Not bad, at his age... And the garden? Of
course, the roses would be over... Could he bring
them anything from London? Just himself... Kind
of her to say so, he would look forward to seeing
them...

Driving through the Surrey countryside, Kemp was
reminded of the many times he had come to Fairlawns in the company of the Gillorns' niece, Penelope Marsden. Now that that chapter had closed, and
Penelope was married to a nice, middle-aged consultant in Norwich, Kemp's visits had been curtailed. Archie had felt some constraint, perhaps even
a measure of embarrassment, for he believed it had
been Penelope who had broken off the relationship
whereas her aunt, who was more shrewd in such
matters, knew better.

It was Florence who greeted him on the steps of the
verandah and for a moment they both stood look-

ing at the low autumn sun sinking beyond the fair gardens which gave the house its name.

'He always likes to see you, Lennox. You've stayed away too long.'

It was only after dinner when Florence said she had things to do elsewhere and left the two men to their port that Archie broached the subject of the Courtenay Trust. The old devil, thought Kemp. I should have guessed.

'Arnold Crayshaw suggested I have a word with you. Said you ought to be put in the picture now that young scallywag Vivian's badgering you...' Archie reached for the decanter with fingers gnarled and swollen.

'It's heavy. Let me...' Kemp poured for them both. 'Can't the doctors do anything for those hands of yours?'

'The ubiquitous palliative pill. Relieves the pain, but don't help me grip things any better.'

'Your grip on things hasn't slackened, you old fraud. You didn't ask me down here to admire your dahlias or talk about rheumatism...' When Lennox Kemp had joined the well-known legal firm of Gillorns in Clement's Inn some six years ago he would never have imagined himself speaking to the senior partner in such terms. Even in retirement the old man was still formidable and Kemp's respect for him undiminished, but it was leavened now by real affection which he knew was reciprocated.

'I'm still a trustee.' The leathery skin was so wrinkled round the hooded eyes that their sharpness was almost hidden in the folds, but Kemp caught a flash of what could only be sardonic glee.

'I thought that Arnold Crayshaw...'

'Appointed when Silas died, but not to replace myself. I may have retired from the practice of law—and thank God for that, the mess they make of it these days—but I hold on to my trusteeships.'

'And Silas was a trustee as well as being a tenant-for-life?'

'A very proper arrangement. A foot in both camps. And he discharged his duties honourably. He improved the legal estate, and he accumulated wealth for the beneficial interest.'

'Sounds a paragon of a man.'

'He was not. Silas was a miser. Getting rich was his only hobby. But he cherished the Courtenay lands, had at least that streak of pride in the old ways... No more port for me. Florence doesn't allow it.' The grating sound as the old man got slowly to his feet could have been a chuckle. 'Must get these creaking bones to bed...'

He brushed off Kemp's helping hand but accepted the rubber-shod stick. 'Take that port into the study, my boy. It's cosier in there, and there's something on my desk you might find of interest. We'll talk in the morning.'

The study, with its dark oak panelling and bookshelves rising to ceiling height, had such a familiar air when he entered it that Kemp smiled to himself. It was a replica—though cleaner—of the senior partner's old room at the London office, even to the vast mahogany desk which he knew had been part of the original furniture when Archie's grandfather had set up his business there over a hundred years ago. The deedbox left open upon it looked not out of place, the white-painted lettering 'Courtenay Trust' almost obliterated by time.

Not even someone in as much of a hurry as Vivian could have hoped to hustle the trustees of such a settlement; they would proceed at the pace of a lethargic snail before they would finally be obliged to hand over those essential symbols of ownership, the title deeds. And here they were to tell the tale of the devolution of Courtenay Manor down the ages, with all its hereditaments and lands, set out in clear copper-plate, or thin spidery handwriting, with many a fanciful curlicue at the corners like marks of feathers stripped from old quill pens.

The vellum crackled under Kemp's eager fingers as he delved into the mass of material, unfolding documents that stretched the breadth of the desk, admiring the embossed stamps with their regnal dates and the crinkled seals hung out with pretty, faded ribbons.

Of more immediate interest, however, were the two documents which he had lifted out first. They were dated September 1926, a Vesting Deed and a Trust Instrument, and as he perused them carefully he found them neither prolix nor unnecessarily complicated; someone had been sure of his own mind and intention. Silas James Courtenay, as absolute owner of the fee simple in possession had vested the property in himself as tenant-for-life upon the trusts set out in the accompanying deed. All had been done correctly under the Settled Land Act of 1925, and the proper steps taken beforehand to make the transition possible were set out in the preamble.

The estate had previously been entailed. Down the centuries it had passed to each male heir in succession. Some, like Silas himself, had been prudent caretakers, others had wasted the assets, run up debts, stripped the land of trees, mortgaged the Manor or let it fall into ruin, and generally played merry hell with their inheritance. In 1926 Silas had barred the entail, which, as tenant-in-tail, he was entitled to do without requiring anyone else's consent; his father was dead by then and there was no protector of the original settlement.

What a field day the lawyers must have had! Kemp sipped his port and thought of the scurrying about when the new reforming property legislation had come upon them. Some lazy landowners would do nothing, hoping it would all go away, but Silas Courtenay had not been one of these; he'd been right on the ball. The estate had not been in very good nick when it had come to his hands at his father's death but a glance through the accounts showed that from then on things had changed for the better. Leases were granted, the cottages and Dower House repaired, the lands put under good husbandry, reafforestation carried out, and the Manor itself restored.

Kemp scrutinized the Trust Deed. Four trustees of the settlement had been appointed, Silas himself and three others, one of whom was Archie Gillorn. Death had taken its toll, and he was the last of the original trustees. Power had been given to appoint others, and a recent document confirmed Arnold Crayshaw as one of them. The trusts themselves were clear enough, no room for ambiguity: the whole estate to be held for Silas's younger brother, Charles Courtenay and his heir in tail male—the latter, now archaic, words presumably inserted by lawyers not yet quite at home with the new Act. As Charles was dead, and Silas too had now been gathered in, the estate in all its entirety would devolve upon Vivian Courtenay.

There were the usual clauses giving the trustees power to expend moneys from the income of the trust fund for the education and maintenance of the beneficiaries—clauses rather more strict than they would be in a more modern deed—while they remained infants, and further provision when they attained their majority, together with benefits for other of Charles's children and portions for any daughters on marriage.

Well, Kemp thought, that accounts for Rugby and Benenden... But after that? No special provisions on their coming of age except for a continuance of allowances—to be at the discretion of the trustees. For the high-spirited and high-spending twins, such allowances must have seemed meagre reward. Of course Vivian could have borrowed heavily against his expectations; after all, his interest under the trust vested when he became twenty-one. And Venetia? She would have her portion on marriage—perhaps it was what Proby had married her for...

All this speculation was purely academic; Vivian had come into his inheritance and the Trust was at an end. Presumably, as the twins were so close, Venetia could expect to share in her brother's good fortune. What must have irked the pair of them woefully was the unconscionable time Silas had taken in dying... Obviously this had not been foreseen when the strict settlement had been set up long before they were born. But why was the estate to devolve on the younger Charles in the first place?

Kemp put the deeds and documents back in the order he had found them, and decided to ask Archie Gillorn the next day.

'Had a good look, did you?' The old gentleman was very spry this morning. 'Thought you might. Of course it's no business of yours but when you're dealing with any of the Courtenays it's as well to look at their history.'

'Why'd Silas not leave the property to his own heirs? He would be about thirty in 1926. He could have married and had children...'

'Silas was what used to be called "delicate". Had been from a boy. When he tried to join the army in 1916 it was discovered he had tuberculosis in both lungs. They talk about cancer now... and this new thing, Aids... people forget what a scourge TB was then. It sounded the death knell for many a youngster. Silas knew he'd never marry; the doctors—gloomy lot they were—gave him only a few years to live. The entail on the Courtenay property would lapse for want of an heir. Then along came the Settled Land Act, and he grabbed at it. All neat and tidy. Brother Charles was young, handsome and healthy, bound to get married and have children. On the expected early demise of Silas, Charles would inherit and hold the estate in trust for his own eldest son. That way Silas did what he could to keep Courtenay Manor in the family—as far as the modern law of real property allowed.'

'But things didn't work out as he planned?'

'Man proposes, God disposes,' said Archie, piously, 'And Silas was a great believer in the Almighty...'

'It was Charles who died, and Silas who went on living?'

'In those days Silas spent much of his time in sanatoriums. There was one up near Aberdeen for a while, and then he was advised to try a clinic in Switzerland. Ye'll have read *The Magic Mountain*?'

Kemp nodded.

'Made a great impression on Silas Courtenay. If Thomas Mann could survive, so could he. Took years, of course. He had relapses, but in the end he was cured. He was over forty by then.'

'And in the meantime Charles had died?'

'A tragedy for all concerned. He never even saw his children. Blanche was carrying the twins when the accident happened.'

'Quite a melodramatic sequence,' observed Kemp. 'Did you know Charles Courtenay?'

'Only by repute. A fast-moving young man, I understand. All over the place. Had a pretty decent war, and ended up in the States. He'd been engaged to Blanche for years, of course. Let me see, now... That would be about 1946 he came home and married her at last. Killed the same year, up grouse-shooting in Scotland...'

It was over lunch at Fairlawns that Kemp returned to the subject of the Courtenays. Florence had been talking about marriage in general with many a sly sidelong glance at himself which he was doing his best to avoid. It would be safer to turn the conversation.

'There was a big difference in age, wasn't there, between Silas Courtenay and his brother Charles?' he said to Archie.

'That's why Silas looked on him more as a son than a brother. Isabella Courtenay was eighteen when Silas was born. She had Charles when she was thirty-eight, and quite a number of sickly infants must have died before then. You have to hand it to those old Victorian families, they kept on trying.'

'They'd be consumptive,' said Florence, knowingly, 'passed on with the mother's milk.'

'Isabella lived on to a ripe old age,' said Archie drily, 'she'd the Dower House till she died, and then it went to Blanche. Silas conceded that much.'

'There was no other provision for Blanche?'

'It was not in the Trust,' said the old man simply. 'She had some Daubeny money when she married but that all went on dubious horse-trainers and handsome grooms. A very silly woman, Blanche. Silas was as generous to her as his nature allowed but he never understood or liked her. Some unfortunate remark she'd made once in his hearing about a broken-winded nag being good for nothing. He thought she was referring to his lungs...'

Florence winced. 'If you two are going to talk about such things I shall go and help Marie with the next course.'

'Was the Trust irrevocable?' Kemp asked when she had gone.

'You should know better than to ask. You've seen it—no power of revocation,' said Archie sternly. 'I suppose a Deed of Arrangement could have been made, but Silas wouldn't have it. It must be as God willed, he said. God had meant him to set up the Trust, and God had wrought the miracle of his cure. Besides, by then Silas was a confirmed bachelor, there would be no heir through him. But he'd not wasted the long years of his illness. In Switzerland—where better?—he'd studied international finance and banking, he made wise investments, played the markets, found he had the flair. He bought and ran various business ventures, ending up with that timber firm...'

'And all the while keeping an eye on the Courtenay estate?'

'A sacred trust—ordained by God. His two passions came together there, the making of money and the preservation of property.'

Kemp moved restlessly. 'He must have been disappointed in his nephew and niece?'

'He did not comment. Meetings of the trustees were formal. Strict adherence to the exact wording of the Deed. Education, yes, maintenance, yes, but any further provision scrutinized and severely curtailed.'

'But, surely, when they were twenty-one?'

The old man sighed. 'You have to remember that Silas was a Victorian. During the years of entail on the estate there had been spendthrift sons, runaway daughters. These things haunted Silas... Vivian by that time had wasted any talent he had, he was running up debts, tailors' bills, fancy cars he couldn't afford on his allowance, trying to keep up with a raffish society...'

'And Venetia?'

'Just as bad—though she did make one attempt at a career. Wanted to go to drama school. Silas wouldn't hear of it. Put his foot down hard. No,

Lennox, those two were living the life of the rich on the strength of their expectations. Neither of them saw fit to work.' The wise old eyes squinted up at Kemp. 'And don't give me any of that broken home, deprived childhood, inadequate mother nonsense you plead in court. The Courtenay twins had an income any middle-class youngster might envy.'

Kemp was aware that he should not reveal more personal curiosity to someone as astute as Archie Gillorn, yet he could not resist probing—like a tongue to an aching tooth. 'I suppose Venetia got her portion when she married Lewis Proby?'

'Proby?' The old man was temporarily distracted. 'If we must imitate Blanche and talk only of horses, I'd say he's a dark one. Can't make him out. Of course he married her in the hope that she was an heiress. He knew something of Silas Courtenay's personal fortune—heard it around the gossipmongers in the City, I've no doubt.' It was as if they inhabited the old coffee-houses, though wine bars would be more appropriate now.

'Courtenay's personal fortune,' repeated Kemp. 'I did wonder about that. None of my business, as you've said, and I presume there was a will.'

'Made at the same time as the settlement,' said Archie promptly, 'and never altered.' He saw Kemp's look of surprise.

'Well, he had no other real estate that was not already in the Trust, and his personalty was to go to Charles and his heirs. Not in equal shares, of course, the largest part ear-marked for the eldest son. He would intend it for the upkeep of the Manor. In 1926 Silas's fortune was not large . . .'

'But he kept pouring it into the Trust fund as time went on?'

'For him it would be the natural thing. He himself lived abstemiously—he'd no option with his disease—and latterly he lived like a recluse in the Manor, spending only what was necessary for repairs and on his own household staff and gardeners.'

Put in plain terms, it sounded reasonable but there were aspects which puzzled Kemp.

'Silas could not have been pleased by the behaviour of his heirs . . .'

'He took a stern view but nothing would make him change either the Trust deed or his will. They were made when he thought he only had a few years to live. God, in his wisdom, granted him nearly sixty. Silas would never question God's purpose.'

Kemp closed his eyes briefly.

'One can only hope,' he said fervently at last, 'that Silas Courtenay lies quiet in Abraham's bosom. Vivian's plans include a permanent site for rock festivals, a roller-skating rink, camping grounds, wargames in the woods, a motorcycle scramble course, and letting the Manor out to a film company.'

Archie Gillorn took it calmly; his part of Surrey was peaceful and a long way from Newtown.

'I wonder what is God's opinion on pop music,' he mused, while slowly dissecting a pear which Florence had peeled for him. 'Sorry to keep harping on the Almighty but he did enter every conversation I ever had with Silas.'

As Archie seemed to have slipped into a meditative phase and might not be too sharply aware, Kemp hazarded another question.

'How well does Venetia Courtenay come out of this? Financially, I mean.'

The old man was concentrating on removing the core. 'She has had advances on her share, I believe, from time to time. She had wheedling ways with Silas, though hc barred her stupid idea of taking to the stage.' He stopped, and Kemp waited. When the fruit had been eaten, piece by piece, Archie remarked: 'They tell me there should be only forty minutes from the time you take a pear from the tree to the time it is enjoyed. The ripeness is all.' He chuckled. 'There is a hotch-potch clause in the will. Silas left nothing to chance. He very nearly made us put in a restraint on anticipation.'

Kemp laughed with him. 'To guard the helpless female from the influence of a grasping husband. That's as out of date as whalebone stays. He should have met some of my female clients! Anyway, I don't see Venetia being unduly influenced by someone as ineffectual as Proby.'

It was an unfortunate remark to have made. Kemp had momentarily forgotten just how astute the old gentleman could be.

'What's this about Venetia and Proby, as you call them? I thought it was Vivian Courtenay who was your client?'

'Their interests might overlap,' was all Kemp could think of to say, and that lamely. 'The brother and sister are very close.'

Archie was wiping his hands on his crumpled table-napkin, a ritual his twisted fingers performed with difficulty. 'What d'ye mean by that? You seem to have got yourself pretty close to one of them.'

'I've met them all, yes.' Kemp realized that Archie had suddenly become disturbed, irritable. 'I meant no more than that.' He was aware that Florence was shaking her head mutely at him from across the table.

'And you've been listening to the gossip, eh?' That bark of Gillorn's could still make one jump.

'Of course I haven't. I don't go in for gossip.'

'Huh! You used to base your cases on it. I know when you're trailing your coat, Lennox. You can't fool me. All this talk of Venetia Courtenay—and on first name terms! You're more interested in that female than in her brother's imbecile plans.' The old man pushed his chair back as if the meal and the discussion were at an end.

'Lennox hasn't finished his coffee,' Florence murmured reprovingly.

'Well, I've finished mine. I'm going for my nap.'
Archie got to his feet, looked for his stick, and took
it from Kemp's hand without so much as a glance, or
word of acknowledgement, and stood glaring at
them both.

It was to Florence he spoke. 'Make him see sense.
You know him as well as I do.'

His wife's eyes had widened. 'What do you want
me to say to him, Archie? What do you want me to
tell him?'

'Oh, tell him what you like! I want no part of it.'

The old man stumped across the floor to the study
door. Kemp opened the door for him, and then returned to the table, bewildered by the interchange
between the Gillorns. How often had he heard the
senior partner say these words: 'I want no part of it.'
When anything had come up of a subversive nature
or insalubrious from a moral standard, Archie Gillorn always ducked from under. This time he seemed
to be leaving things to his wife.

'What on earth have I said to upset him?'

Florence busied herself replenishing their coffee
cups. 'Archie gets irritated easily—well, more easily
than he used to.'

'But all we were doing was talking about the
Courtenay Trust, and that's why I was asked down,
wasn't it?'

Florence smiled. 'Not entirely, Lennox. He always wants to see you, perhaps that was just an excuse. He still feels badly about Penelope.'

'But that's all over. And you know it was never meant to be.'

'I knew that, but Archie still thinks she let you down and that as a result you're vulnerable.'

Kemp was amazed. 'What, me? A once-bitten, twice-shy, lawyer with a case-load of crooks and crumby divorces!'

'Don't joke, Lennox. I think it's your women clients he worries about sometimes. He thinks you might have been left bitter by Penelope's marriage to another man.' She sounded amused. 'I know you better than that. Archie is rather old-fashioned in some ways, he can't help imagining that you might, well, be taken in by some unscrupulous woman. There, I've said it. I know how silly it is . . .'

Kemp threw back his head and laughed. But he sobered quickly as he realized there might be a serious implication. 'Archie is worried that it could be Venetia Courtenay?'

'You have met her?'

'She rather sought me out,' said Kemp cautiously, finding that it was true.

'And you have been inclined to push the conversation in her direction,' Florence said primly. 'I try not to listen but I can't help hearing. And I can guess when you have a woman on your mind.'

Feminine intuition could make a man nervous— particularly if his conscience was not clear nor his feelings unengaged.

'I have only seen the lady in question twice, Florence, and have thought little of her since. She's a sight too highly-born for me. Besides, she's married.'

'That's no barrier these days,' said Florence robustly. 'But there's something else... You know I've never had anything to do with Archie's legal matters, nor ever wanted to, but once he had retired there was no longer the same need for secrecy and he has tended to share any anxieties he has. One of these has been this awful Trust. He'd have given it up years ago if he hadn't promised Mr Silas.'

'Why should the Trust cause Archie anxiety?'

'Well, he was asked to keep an eye on the beneficiaries for Mr Silas, not just their finances but their private lives... Archie hated doing it—you know how he loathes any kind of spying. But it was a duty put upon him by Silas Courtenay, and Archie couldn't shirk it, no matter how unpleasant—even if it only meant listening...'

'Listening to what?' Kemp prompted her gently.

'To the rumours that were going about. What was being said on all sides wherever the Courtenay twins travelled. That they were too close to one another... And it didn't stop when Venetia got married...' Florence gave a sharp little movement of the head. 'Don't make me use the word, Lennox.'

She didn't need to. Kemp remembered all too well the brotherly hand on the white shoulder; he had thought then it was possessive, excluding any other.

The word was still taboo even in these enlightened times... No, he wouldn't expect Florence to speak it. For himself, it was as if he'd touched the raw end of a high-voltage wire.

'Did Archie tell Silas Courtenay of these rumours?'

Florence met Kemp's eyes frankly now, as if she had been relieved of a burden. 'No. And I'm glad he didn't. To give a man like Mr Silas such unwelcome news would have killed him.'

Perhaps that was what was meant. Kemp hastily thrust the fleeting thought from him as being irrational, but the suspicion lingered. What had rationality to do with dark impulses that might breed in the close ties of birth, the nearness in blood? Hadn't he himself wondered whether Vivian and Venetia were warped by the frustrations of their waiting years? But mere cupidity was clean compared to this...

He became aware that Florence was looking at him expectantly and, as if from a long way off, it came back to him that there had been a reason for this conversation.

'You can set Archie's mind at rest. I've no intention of getting in any way involved with Venetia Proby. But thank him for the warning,' he added impishly, 'I can see why he dodged out of it. As for Mr Vivian Courtenay, well, many of my clients have darker secrets but unless they're thinking of blowing up Parliament, they're none of my business.'

That, at least, succeeded in making Florence laugh.

SEVEN

DRIVING BACK TO Newtown on the Sunday night
Kemp's thoughts during the journey were nothing
like so tranquil as they had been on the drive down.
Then they had been of the past, pleasantly nostalgic
and by no means regretful. Now they were of the future, and darkened by misgivings. He hated having
his emotional equilibrium thrown out of joint. One
of the consolations of travelling alone was that he
could retreat into the small kingdom of his head
without interference by outside influences if he chose
to ignore them. He would now dearly like to ignore
the Courtenays.

It was a nonsense, he told himself sternly, to
imagine he was personally affected by what Florence had revealed, the gist of it confirmed by Archie
Gillorn in a subsequent conversation, strained as
through a sieve by the old man's reticence. He had
gruffly apologized for his temper after lunch and
hoped that Kemp had not taken it amiss. Kemp could
only make awkward noises of dissent while assuring
his host that the confidence permitted him would be
respected.

'Confidence be damned. It's no matter now. I was
the only one kept my mouth shut. D'ye think I did

right?' The glance from under the heavy eyelids was piercing as an eagle's.

After only a moment's hesitation Kemp had answered him. 'I'd have done the same, Archie. From what you've told me of Silas Courtenay, he was convinced he was fulfilling God's wish. If he'd learned anything from you of this—aberrant behaviour— he'd have been forced to take a long hard look at the purposes of God. And, perhaps, it was only talk...'

Archie had lowered his eyes, retracting his head on its bony neck like a tortoise going back into its shell, a habit he had when it was his wish to terminate a discussion.

'Then we shall add nothing further to it.'

The Courtenays had not been referred to again for the rest of Kemp's stay at Fairlawns. Hardly surprising, he thought sardonically, as he put his car in the garage: the taint of an unnatural relationship between a known brother and sister would be a conversation-stopper even in the most liberated company. With elderly, upright people like the Gillorns it would die on the breath—as it had done on Florence's.

Kemp was annoyed at his own state of mind, at the tide of conflicting emotions now surging about inside him and which he would gladly have thrown out like so much dirty dishwater. He had a busy week ahead of him for which he required a clear head, and a good night's sleep.

As it was he slept badly, and woke in no better mood. Over breakfast he took a firm resolve to prise loose from his memory all those tantalizing images of Venetia Courtenay or Proby which kept on reappearing as if she was becoming an obsession. Kemp knew all about obsessions; far too many of his clients were bedevilled by them. If he could not forget Venetia he could at least rationalize her away; try to explain to himself just where the attraction lay. It was all to do with what he had lightly called her highborn status—and those long pale looks from aristocratic eyes.

You're a fool, he told himself as he buttered his burnt toast, but at least you're beginning to see the light; the lure lies not in Venetia herself as a female person of considerable beauty, but in her class. Satisfied with this deduction, he went on to drink his coffee. After all, he argued, he had felt it from the first when his thoughts had run to servile states and feudal rights . . .

Of course he ought now to be feeling repugnance. . . Even that was not clear-cut; there had been one awful moment in the night when he had felt himself drawn to her in a different, quite alarming, way. Was it simple fascination with the idea of evil, an innate curiosity about the springs of corruption, not a prurient interest but a real desire to comprehend the nature of perversion?

As he hurriedly threw papers into his briefcase, locked the flat and went to the garage for his car—

the normal everyday drill—such reflections pursued him and were still in attendance as he bounded up the stairs to his office.

Elvira had sorted the mail, and it lay ready on his desk. Going through it restored his calm of mind and would have allowed him to give his full attention to his work had it not been for a thick white envelope addressed to himself and marked 'private'. He slit the envelope and took out the deckle-edged card embossed in gold.

Mr Lennox Kemp was invited to a Masquerade and Mediaeval Banquet at Courtenay Manor on November 5th. Turning it over, he saw that she had written: 'Do come, Lennox, it's our Birthdays!!!'

He was still staring at it, uncertain whether it pleased or frightened him, when Elvira came in.

''Morning, Mr Kemp. You were late so I did the mail... I've got something very odd to tell you.' She was bobbing up and down with excitement.

'You've got another job.' It was an old joke between them.

'Don't be silly. Do you remember the Sorrento kid, the one who swallowed the ink?'

'Not something to forget in a hurry.'

'Well, I saw him on Saturday. At the playground in Wellington Park.'

Kemp was hardly listening. Did he really want to go to this masquerade thing? He propped the invitation up against the bulk of the Law List, and read the flamboyant print again. Really, it was all in the most execrable taste...

'Did you hear what I said, Mr Kemp? I saw Luke Sorrento.'

'But he's in Sicily... Oh well, I suppose they might have come back.'

'That's not the point. He wasn't with her. Not the Mrs Sorrento who came in here...'

The telephone rang, and Kemp took it up. A builder wanted to know if those leases were ready.

'Blackburns, Elvira? Are the papers ready for signature?'

'Of course they are. The engrossments were all typed on Friday afternoon, like you said.'

'Yes, Mr Blackburn, they're ready. Can you come in this morning? Right, I'll see you at eleven.' He put the phone down. 'Give me an hour, Elvira. What other appointments have I got today?'

'Mrs Stewart's coming in at ten, and the Browns at half-past...'

'Squeeze Blackburn in at eleven. It shouldn't take long. I'm in Court at twelve but it's only asking for adjournment. Mr Cantley wants me for a meeting at two-thirty so the afternoon looks pretty busy... Hop off now, there's a good girl and bring me the Blackburn file.'

'Mr Kemp... if you'd only listen...'

'Later, Elvira, later.'

Elvira considered it was not ladylike to flounce, but she closed the door with a snap.

The rush of work continued for most of the day and it was only when she came in for the signed mail at five-thirty that she had the chance to speak to him again.

'I wanted to tell you about those Sorrento children. I really did see them...'

'What? Sorry, I don't know that it matters. Anyway, how do you know it was the Sorrento family?'

'That's the whole point. It wasn't.' Elvira in her exasperation was getting incoherent. 'Not the whole family, I mean.'

The invitation card, looking more ostentatious than ever, was still on his desk. How did one reply to a thing like that, he wondered?

He became aware that Elvira was waiting impatiently. 'You know I'm not very good with children,' he said with a smile. 'I wouldn't really remember them, and you only saw them for a few minutes.'

'I wasn't sure myself, not at first, but then the boy saw me and pulled a face... just like that...' Elvira drew down her lower lip and pointed a finger inside her grimacing mouth. 'He remembered me all right.'

Kemp went on signing his letters. He wasn't really interested in what Elvira was saying. All this bother about kids. Perhaps she was considering having some herself; he'd be sorry to lose her if that were so...

'But when I went over to him, the woman just grabbed him and rushed off. Then I saw the little girl was with them too. They were all gone out of the playground before I could catch up with them.'

'Probably took you for a social worker, Elvira. Those kind of people tend to run at the sight of one.' He spoke absently, his eyes again on the card in front of him.

'What do you mean by those kind of people? You didn't used to talk like that, Mr Kemp.' She glanced down to see what had absorbed his attention. 'Was that what came for you this morning? My word, you are moving into high society!' She picked up the folder of mail. 'I just don't know what to do about those children . . .'

'Who? Oh, the ones you saw in the park. Well, they're probably being minded by someone . . . Before you leave, Elvira, would you please inquire of Frank what he's done with that company formation I asked him to deal with.'

Elvira gave up. 'Yes, Mr Kemp,' she said sulkily, 'and good night.'

He thought she sounded a bit put out, but she was probably in a hurry to get home.

How like the Courtenays to give a mediaeval banquet! That would be Vivian's idea, the new Lord of the Manor out to impress the people of Newtown. But it was she who had written the personal message . . . He could not think now of one without the other, and that line of thought led downwards into thorn bushes . . .

He wondered if Lettice Warrender had been asked.

'WE BOTH HAVE,' she told him when he met her several days later. 'John's not at all keen. Says it sounds a lot of pretentious nonsense. Nice of you to offer me lunch, Lennox. What do you want this time?'

They were settled in a comfortable booth in the Cabbage White.

'Why, the pleasure of your company, my dear Letty. Since when have I had ulterior motives?'

'Since as long as I've known you.' Lettice had few illusions about her amiable friend. 'As all your builder clients seem to be in seventh heaven over recent Council decisions, I assume it's not for business reasons you seek me out...'

'Eat up your lasagne like a nice girl, and have some white wine.'

'How lavish you are. And on a weekday, too!'

It was true that Kemp enjoyed Lettice Warrender's company—though there were times when her bubbling energy and youthful enthusiasms made him feel aged and indolent. Her warm delight in his had the opposite effect.

She chose a chocolate éclair, and licked cream from her fingers as she chattered. 'Dad and Mother have received an invitation to this thing at the Manor too. Can't think why, it'll be ever so boisterous and Mother'll hate it. There's to be fireworks over the lake later on. Mother thinks it's all frightfully bad taste.'

Kemp could hear her say it. Mrs Warrender's ideas about how one should conduct oneself in society had been well-founded on Lady Troubridge, and were now set hard like concrete.

'Will they go?' asked Kemp.

'They might. Dad says he wants to have a quiet talk with Lewis Proby. They seem to have some interest in common... Dad's in for a shock if the party's anything like the last one. He'll have to yell at the top of his voice just to say hello... Are you going to dress up, Lennox?'

'I haven't said I'm going yet, and I am certainly not going to dress up.'

Lettice regarded him with half-closed eyes. 'I see you in a sort of grey habit. A monk, but worldly.'

'Friar Tuck? Thank you, Lettice, that's made my day.'

'Seriously. Do come with us. It might be fun. John can talk fetlocks with Blanche Courtenay while you and I flirt outrageously with each other.'

'There'll be headlines in the papers next day: Local Lawyer Laid Low by Vengeful Vet... Not even for you, Letty. John's bigger than me and he could fell an ox.'

'He doesn't get much practice. Newtowners seem content with smaller mammals for pets, but he was ever so pleased to get that contract with Amy's riding school. You did it, didn't you, Lennox?'

'I may have mentioned his name to both Mrs Francis and Mrs Courtenay.'

That had been the only good result to come out of Kemp's visit to the Gillorns. He had told Archie of

the project, and the old man must have bent Arnold
Crayshaw's ear backwards, for the money had been
paid to Blanche and the partnership agreement duly
signed.

'Mrs Courtenay actually called on Mother last
week,' said Lettice, 'wanted to renew the friendship.
Not that there'd ever been much of one in the first
place. Mother was very impressed. Even said she was
sorry for Blanche.'

Kemp knew that Paula Warrender's fount of
sympathy ran fairly shallow so he was interested to
know why. It seemed that now she had left the Dower
House Blanche intended to make a new life for herself and do useful work in the community. He remarked that that did not sound like the old Blanche
Courtenay.

'It's because she's escaped at last from that awful
family of hers,' said Lettice knowingly, 'and not before time . . .'

'You're talking about the twins? Why're they so
awful?'

Lettice looked at him with wide eyes; she had
learned a lot since joining the local bureaucracy. 'So
that's why you asked me to lunch! You want my
opinion of Viv and Venetia?'

It had been almost exactly that, but Lennox Kemp
was an old hand at this game; when your position is
unstable, you attack.

'It was you, remember, who got me mixed up with
them in the first place, and now I've been honoured

by this second invitation. I want to know a lot more about these people. I just don't go anywhere, you know, I'm a very exclusive person.'

Lettice burst out laughing, but she realized that he was serious and, anyway, she knew he was owed some kind of explanation.

'It's true Venetia did ask me to bring you especially to that party. It wasn't because John was away. I still can't figure out why she wanted to meet you. She said it was because Viv needed a new lawyer but I just don't believe it. Those two have always had plenty of legal wallahs to get them out of scrapes... They got drunk and crashed their car in Paris once, so someone had to go over and bail them out. Viv got into some brawl when they were in Italy and Venetia wouldn't leave him, so off goes another family lawyer to rescue them both. They were forever running out of funds abroad and phoning up their mother in the middle of the night to make her get more money out of Uncle Silas... The tales are endless, Lennox.' By now Lettice's face was pink. 'I know I don't sound very nice about them and they're supposed to be my friends...'

'Well, I did ask for your opinion...'

'I shouldn't have got carried away like that.' Lettice's voice was muffled. 'I suppose you've concluded I don't like the Courtenay twins.'

Kemp smiled. 'Something like that. But you'll go to their banquet?'

'You do make me sound rotten. It's just that...
Well, I did like Venetia when we were at school, even
though she scared me a bit. I never really liked Vivian at all.' Lettice looked out of the window, the colour still high on her cheeks, but she saw herself as a
modern young woman, not one to shirk an issue. 'As
a matter of fact, I used to think he might be gay.
Now I'm not so sure. There's something not quite
right about him, though... But it's when they're together it's so awful, the way they play up to each
other. They've always done it, right from when they
were children, but now it seems to have got worse.
John and I saw them in the supper bar of the Cam-
berwell Beauty last Saturday night and they came
over. Their behaviour was quite...well, bizarre.'

Lettice pursed her lips in a way which reminded
Kemp of her mother. You're not as emancipated as
you like to think, young lady, he nearly commented,
but wisely did not.

She was fumbling under her chair for her handbag. 'Just look at the time! This gossiping... I ought
to be ashamed of myself. It's all your fault, Lennox
Kemp, you have a terrible way of drawing people
out... Well, for that, you can jolly well come with
John and me to the banquet. Promise?'

'I promise. But, definitely no fancy dress.'

'OK.' Lettice had recovered herself. 'If you be-
have improperly, which I hope you will, I'll show you
the dungeon.'

'What dungeon? There aren't any dungeons at Courtenay Manor, it's all on the level.' Kemp had taken a look at the many scrolls of plans in the deedbox, and knew there was nothing below ground shown in any of them.

'It's not a proper dungeon. Viv and Venetia used to call it that when we went up to the Manor to play in the holidays. It's where that French prisoner was kept. I must go. I'll tell you the story when we meet on the fifth. How like the twins to be born on Guy Fawkes' Night!'

EIGHT

FRANK FOSDYKE, Kemp's articled clerk, was young and relatively inexperienced despite having an excellent degree. He rather fancied himself, in the future, as a wily negotiator in City financial circles advising multinationals on takeover bids and mergers. At present, however, he was only at the alphabet stage in company law, and he put the file marked V. & V. Enterprises on Kemp's desk with the air of a bright schoolboy given too easy an exercise.

'So that's all there is to it? You just buy an existing company that's gone bust, and change the name?'

'Dead simple, the way you put it,' said Kemp, 'but let's see what you've got.' He took out the Articles of Association and went through the names. 'That's it... Mr Courtenay and Mrs Proby are the directors, Mr Lewis Proby is the secretary, and the registered office is Courtenay Manor. Now for the Memorandum. I told you what the objects were: the promotion and provision of entertainment, leisure facilities and sports. These clauses look all right, Frank, they seem to cover every activity for man and muscle—not a lot for the mind, perhaps, but we're not talking about the Arts Council... Wouldn't put it past Mr Vivian Courtenay to try and stretch them into running a brothel or gambling casino—there's money in both. And I gather he's got the shooting rights tied up anyway.'

'He's likely to find himself looking down the wrong end of a gun if the people of Newtown have their way,' remarked Frank, with some asperity. 'A lot of them are up in arms about his proposals. They say they like being surrounded by quiet green fields.'

Kemp gave a hoot of laughter. He was tickled by the idea of Newtown being packed with conservationists, and said so. 'Newtown's come a bit late to the not-in-my-backyard syndrome... You've done a good job on this, Frank. Have you asked our clients to come in?'

'This afternoon, four o'clock. Here's the seal, by the way, and I've checked with the Companies Registry—the name's OK.'

Whether by accident or design—and Kemp suspected it was deliberately contrived—the Courtenay twins arrived for their appointment dressed in almost brazenly identical fashion but without either of them having betrayed their sex. Vivian's sporting outfit in Lovat green had darker green velvet at the collar which matched Venetia's velvet suit; the cream silk frill of her cuffs and the jabot at her throat harmonized perfectly with the cream of his cotton shirt.

No green wellies, though. Kemp, who was keeping his head down, watched the progress of their feet across his rug and decided that both pairs of highly-polished shoes must have been cut out of the same poor crocodile's hide.

The heads, too, were equally well-groomed as if set for a double portrait, his longish hair brushed carelessly back to hide thinning on the high forehead, hers a smooth cap of shining gold secured at the base of her neck by an outlandish great bow of black satin. That, and the creamy fall of silk at her chin, gave her the look of a Jacobean dandy—and she obviously knew it.

Indeed, both Vivian and Venetia once seated and leaning slightly towards each other seemed poised as if to take part in a play. Restoration comedy perhaps, Kemp reckoned, holding fast to a sardonic sense of humour which might well be the only thing to save him from the impact of her silvery eyes.

Today they were cool and haughty; she was being the businesswoman. She wasn't bad at it, either. More attentive than her brother, who was restless, bored by the paperwork and a deal more subdued than on his previous visit. He only flickered into life when she pulled his string. The banter between them was carried on in a private language, charged with subtle elements which had echoes of the schoolroom, or even further back, the nursery. There were other intimations. Vivian was uneasy, he kept stretching out his long legs, examining his socks for flaws, and generally giving the impression that he would rather be somewhere else.

'These are the company books, and the seal, Mrs Proby. They should be kept by your husband, of course. If you will let me know where he can be reached, I'll get in touch.'

She took out a card and handed it across the desk. A firm of City stockbrokers, known to Kemp, and in the corner, Mr Lewis Proby.

'You have your ear to the ground, Kemp,' said Vivian languidly. 'Heard any buzz from the local planning moguls?'

Kemp certainly had, much of it not for Vivian Courtenay's hearing.

'I don't know about the County,' he said cautiously, 'but the locals might look favourably on a golf-course, or a decent upmarket hotel. I think these were your suggestions, Mrs Proby?'

'But we've changed our minds, haven't we, Viv?'

'I hate golf. All these silly old buffers puttering around... Anyway, it costs the earth to lay out... And I don't want a bloody hotel. Pop festivals bring in the money, and you don't even need to cut the grass.'

Kemp tried to convey something of the sensitive nature, the tender susceptibilities of planning committees. 'They're allergic to any noise that doesn't actually come from machinery or motor-cars,' he explained, 'and whatever your taste in music, rock festivals do mean noise.'

'With all our broad acres?' Venetia's laugh was contemptuous. 'And don't think the youth of Newtown won't come running at the first beat of a drum!'

Kemp had to admit she had a point. They were shrewder than they looked, the Courtenays, they'd gauged the mood of the place. Local teenagers would flock to any new sound from their pop music idols, and Vivian was prepared to pay for the best as he reeled off a list of names and groups. Kemp wondered how they were all thought up, these freaky little spurts of wit and whimsy written down on disk and record sleeve; how long before apt words ran out and they had to start over again... He knew his mind was wandering, and was relieved when Venetia said: 'Oh, shut up, Viv. Mr Kemp isn't interested in your scene.'

'It'll bring in the shekels, Sis,' said her brother, sulkily. 'I've got the record companies interested even if Kemp isn't... And, anyway, my associates will deal with planning applications to the County, then we can tackle the locals.'

'Theme parks are all the rage nowadays,' Kemp remarked casually, determined to ignore Vivian's rudeness. He quoted a member of the Development Corporation who was fired by the notion of the Courtenay estate as a nature reserve and historical treasure-house for the edification of Newtown's schoolchildren. 'After all, your Uncle Silas took great pains to restore the Elizabethan wing.'

'History's boring and unnecessary,' Vivian burst out. 'God, the place was stuffy enough when the old man was there. I won't have the Manor turned into a museum. I want people to have fun. I know lots of chaps in London who'll pay the earth to have a bit of a fling now and again...'

Venetia's eyes were alight with mischief as she leaned over and said to Kemp: 'We're going to hire it out for parties where people can let their hair down. We might advertise it for orgies... Or a meeting-place for some of the weirder cults where everyone takes their clothes off...'

The twins fell back together in paroxysms of clownish laughter which was in no way good-humoured. Kemp fought hard against growing temper, sensing he was the butt of their mockery. It made him more alert to the peculiar chemistry which seemed to work between them and accentuate their worst features. If I had Mr Vivian Courtenay alone, he said fervently to himself, I could take him apart. I might even be able to handle her if I caught her in one of her better moods. But when they're joined like this, they're capable of anything. For the first time he thought of the Courtenay twins as quite danger-ous.

For the sake of saying something, and to show that he too was not without humour, he said: 'I'm sorry you turn down the idea of a theme park, or a high-class hotel. Why not combine the two? You could advertise that wing of the mansion as purely Eliza-bethan. As long as you make sure there's plenty of sprung mattresses in the four-posters, American tourists would come in droves. They love a bit of historical authenticity when they're searching for their ancestors and hoping to find links with the gentry... I mean, it might be a real money-spinner, and that's what you want, isn't it?'

His voice trailed off as he realized that both his listeners had stopped laughing and were regarding him with wary curiosity. He knew he had been drivelling on, talking for the sake of talking, not at all his usual style. The twins had unnerved him with their frivolous approach to problems which were serious enough to others; he could never be certain whether they were taking in what he was saying anyway. Perhaps he shouldn't have mentioned money... All very well for Vivian to have his mind set on raking in the shekels, but it might be seen in bad taste for his legal adviser to be so brutally frank...

My remarks weren't all that witty, Kemp told himself, but my audience might at least have raised a smile between them. Instead, both pairs of eyes had turned coldly upon him as if he were a music-hall comedian whose act had flopped. There was an uncomfortable silence, and as he seemed to be the one who had caused it, he hesitated to break it.

Venetia got to her feet abruptly. She snatched up the handbag she had so precisely placed on the edge of the desk and, for a startled moment, Kemp thought she was going to take a swipe at him with it, but all she said in a voice like ice was:

'Have you got a loo in this place?'

He very nearly retorted, 'No, we go down the street to the public toilets,' but quickly recovered himself and his manners. 'Of course, Mrs Proby, the ladies' room is at the end of the corridor.'

He opened the door for her, and she swept past him, her face pale and tight-lipped. Had he been, quite unwittingly, rude to her too? He shrugged his shoulders. Perhaps she had suddenly felt faint—

though he could not see her as the type to use that Victorian maiden's prerogative. More likely, she simply had a natural need.

Kemp went back to Vivian who was striding up and down the room muttering to himself. Aware of Kemp's inquiring glance, he made an effort to relax, throwing his long body back into his chair with studied nonchalance. Evidently he was prepared to be conciliatory.

'Women!' he exclaimed, very man to man. 'They get their insides in a twist.'

Kemp had not envisaged anyone as patrician as the noble Venetia having insides; he had been more taken up with the outer lineaments...

Vivian was talking about rock festivals again as if he knew it was the one topic of which he had mastery. Kemp was prepared to grant him that, while noting the change in subject. In the absence of his sister Vivian was busy papering over some invisible crack in the earlier conversation. For the life of him Kemp could not remember what it had been about; it all seemed quite irrelevant.

He was trying in vain to pick up lost threads when he realized Vivian had asked him a question and expected an answer.

'What, me? Oh, I'm afraid I never got beyond the Beatles and the Rolling Stones. Child of my times, I am, in that respect... What do I listen to? Well, classical, I suppose...' Then, not wishing to give the impression of being a musical snob, he added hastily: 'But I've always liked folk stuff, Steeleye Span, that kind of thing...'

Vivian approved. 'Good choice,' he said, nodding his head as if to allow that even a lawyer might occasionally exhibit good sense.

Having at last discovered common ground with this scion of the Courtenays, Kemp explored it further, anything was better than to sit in glum silence. 'There's one of their ballads called "Little Sir Hugh"—I've never been able to catch the words properly. Do you know it?'

Vivian obliged by humming a few bars. 'That's it,' exclaimed Kemp, 'the lad goes over the castle wall, and is slain by the lady in green. He's calling for his mother to make his bed. "Make for me a winding sheet..."' Kemp sang the phrase as the words came to him.

Then he stopped. Venetia had come in, unheard, through the door left ajar. She had put on fresh powder and a flick of lipstick.

Vivian scrambled to his feet, and instinctively the twins drew together. She put a hand on his sleeve which creased the tweed. 'What was all that about, Viv?' she said softly.

'It was only a song. Just a song. Seems Kemp has a taste for such things... Come on, Sis, let's get out of here...'

'Well, well, the surprising Mr Kemp.' The mocking tone was back in her voice.

She turned at the door and looked back, a searching look that held both perplexity and inquiry. Even as he met it, head on, it changed and in the silver-green of her eyes he caught the glint of a challenging recklessness.

Kemp leant back in his chair and contemplated the door that had closed behind them. What was that all about, Venetia had asked? He was blessed if he knew. First, the twins had been turned to stone by his lame attempts at wit, then his singing had rendered them speechless. You never set up as an entertainer, he told himself, but at least you used to keep a hold on an audience. You're losing your grip.

Both performances were well outside his normal office behaviour, and for the lapse he could only blame the effect the Courtenays were having on him. They did not see themselves in the usual run of clients, and he for his part had not treated them as such. They were creatures of changing moods, mercurial by temperament, and by that same quicksilver their real personalities slid away from easy recognition. Kemp considered himself fairly expert at discerning character beneath the flummery in which people dressed, the masks and armour to ward off too sharp a scan, but these two defeated him.

Even Vivian, whom he had disliked on sight, appeared now to have a more amiable side; at ease in company which shared his perhaps trivial preoccupations, he could well prove amusing and knowledgeable.

As for Venetia... His thoughts swung away to the morning he had met her in the gardens of the Manor and she had deliberately drawn him to her. *I met a lady in the meads . . .*

There was no telling into what far land those wild, wild eyes might have led his imagination had he not at that moment been interrupted.

Elvira marched in. She was cross, and crosser still to find him doing nothing but stare out of the window.

She put the heavy folder of letters down on the desk in front of him. 'That's the lot. Three whole tapes, Mr Kemp.'

If her tone was not as cold as Venetia's had been it was frosty enough. It spoke of hours at the typewriter while he sat entertaining clients and doodling on his blotting pad. And he knew Elvira better; one look at her flushed face and the disorder in her ginger-blonde hair told him he was again in trouble.

'All right. What's the matter, Elvira?'

She made a great play of pushing back her cuff and looking at her watch. 'There's all that signing to do if the post-girl is to be away by six o'clock . . .' Elvira could be relied upon to keep the essential wheels of the office turning smoothly despite the clogs put on them by others. She had the kind of fair skin which mottled when she was angry. It was mottled now. Kemp sighed.

'I'll sign the mail, but spare me a few moments of your precious time afterwards. You've got something to say and it's better said soon or that red head of yours is going to explode.'

Elvira didn't like being called a redhead, and in fact she did not have the temper supposed to go with the colour. She went out of the room smartly, only just not banging the door.

Kemp went through his outgoing correspondence carefully as he always did, and handed her the folder when she returned. He put his hands behind his head and gave her a quizzical look. 'Am I to have the benefit of some important disclosure?'

'Don't try out your sarcasm on me, Mr Kemp, I'm too ignorant to appreciate it. I'll be back when I've given these to Doreen. You enjoy your peace and quiet. It's hell out there at post-time... Some of us do work, you know.'

That parting shot was as close to insubordination as he'd ever heard from Elvira, who normally kept her place despite their long relationship. It was in her nature to do so. As a typist those long years ago when he'd met her first at Macready's Detective Agency in Walthamstow, she had aspired to being a secretary. Even then she had fixed ideas about what that entailed: you wore dark dresses with white collars, you assumed a ladylike accent, you put only the palest polish on your nails and you never carried your shopping in a string bag.

Waiting for her now to return and spit out whatever it was that was eating her, Kemp cast his mind back to those early days, she then at the start of her career, he at the time disgracefully at the end of his. Or so it had seemed... He'd taken the job as one of the operatives at the Agency when both his marriage and his professional life had fallen apart. Struck off the roll of solicitors by the Law Society for embezzling trust funds to pay for his ex-wife's gambling debts, he'd been lucky to find work of any kind. He realized now that it had been a long time since he'd given a thought to the lean years before his reinstatement and his subsequent success with Gillorns.

Only Elvira remained as a link—and a reminder to himself that he was fallible. All lawyers, he mused now, should have that kind of reminder. It might make them more tolerant of the frailties of their clients. Few people remembered his lapse, although it had never been secret, and Elvira would be the last person to speak of it. She had sympathized with him then, she had been loyal to him since... He was conscious that lately he had given her very little thought. Had he strained that loyalty by taking her for granted?

On an impulse he went to his cabinet and took out a bottle of sherry and two glasses, refreshment he kept for late clients though he rarely indulged in it himself.

It was after six when Elvira came in.

'Sit down and have a sherry. You look as if you've had a hard day.'

'Thank you, Mr Kemp.' She settled herself primly in the chair opposite to him. 'No harder than most.'

'Now, what's the trouble, Elvira?'

She had difficulty in finding the right words. 'I'm not complaining, Mr Kemp...'

'You never do. But something upset you this afternoon?'

A sip of sherry seemed to revive the outrage. 'That Mrs Proby, that... her that calls herself lady of the moor... She bumped right into me in the corridor, knocked a pile of papers out of my hands. Never a word of apology. Just swept on like she was the Queen of Sheba.'

'Even high-born ladies do have to go to the lavatory.'

'High-born! There you go again.' Elvira drained her sherry with a gulp. 'You're so mixed up with that lot out at Courtenay Manor you don't know whether you're coming or going. And you're neglecting the things you ought to be doing.'

This was criticism of a high order, coming as it did from one thoroughly conversant with his work. Kemp was shaken.

'What do you mean by that?'

'There's things need looking into. Oh, I know they're not rich like your new friends, but it isn't like you, Mr Kemp, to ignore them. You never used to be like that. I've often heard you say your legal aid clients deserve as much attention as your fee-paying ones.'

Kemp poured her another sherry. 'You walk home, don't you, Elvira?' he remarked, absently. Was it true what she was saying? He'd certainly spent a lot of time lately up at the planning offices sounding out the officials on the Courtenay schemes ... And that visit to Fairlawns ... There had been other work he should have been doing that weekend. But there must be more to it than that. It was unusual for Elvira to be so hostile to a woman client; Venetia Courtenay had certainly put her back up. A touch of class, perhaps? He dismissed the notion. Elvira always handled that kind of thing with aplomb.

'You don't like Mrs Proby?'

But that was too direct for Elvira. 'I don't like rudeness, Mr Kemp, whoever it comes from,' she said primly. 'It's not my place to have opinions about your clients. All the same, there's something about her... I get the oddest feeling. Oh, I don't know... I'm not quick like you. I've just got a kind of muddled impression...'

Elvira gave herself a little shake, and took a sip of sherry.

'Now, about these legal aid people you say I'm not attending to properly, I suppose it's because I didn't listen to you when you were talking about the Sorrento children a few days ago?'

Elvira nodded vigorously. She put down her glass.

'You weren't interested but I felt I had to do something about it, so I did.'

This time she really had startled him. 'You, Elvira?'

'I've learnt a lot from you, Mr Kemp, when it comes to looking into things. I went back to that playground the following Saturday, and they were there again with the same woman. Not the one who came in here. Anyway, this time I thought I'd make sure she didn't run off, so I gave young Luke a push on the swings, then took his hand and went over to her. She had Maria with her too. Well, this woman was ever so scared at first, but I got her talking. I told her I worked at your office and that's where I'd seen the children first. Mr Kemp, they were her kids!'

'Mrs Sorrento's?' Kemp was as bewildered by the story as by Elvira's method of telling it.

'No, they're this woman's. Her name's Mungo, Annie Mungo, and they're a one-parent family, living on the other end of the caravan site from Mrs Sorrento. She was married to an Italian too, that's why the children look like that, but she divorced him years ago, and now she's on her own. She hardly knew Mrs Sorrento, but sometime in August or September, she can't remember which, Mrs Sorrento came and asked if she could borrow the children.'

'Borrow them?' Kemp exclaimed.

'That's right. Seems she said her husband had gone off, and she had to go to the DHSS and the solicitors, and she'd get more sympathy if the kids were with her. From what Annie Mungo told me that seems to be true—particularly at the Social Services where you mightn't have to wait so long if you've got kids crawling all over you. Annie Mungo says it's been done before so she didn't see any harm in it, just letting the kids go out with Mrs Sorrento for an afternoon, and Mrs Sorrento paid her...'

Kemp held up a hand. 'Stop, Elvira. Give me breathing space while I get this straight. What about Mrs Sorrento's own children?'

'Said they'd gone to her mother's in London, but it was ever so urgent she went to the DHSS to claim her money, and to a solicitor so's they'd trace her husband. It made a sort of sense, the way Mrs Mungo told it.'

'Well, it makes no sort of sense at all for me. Mrs Sorrento told me she'd been to the Social Services first, and they'd sent her on. At least that's what I thought she said. It must be in my notes of the interview.'

Elvira smiled. 'They were a bit scrappy,' she said. 'I've looked them up.'

'The devil you have!' Elvira had turned out to be quite an investigator; her days at Macready's hadn't been wasted. 'And this Mrs Mungo told you she was paid?'

'Oh yes, it was the money that did it. She's ever so badly off, struggling to bring up two kids on her own. She was glad of the money.'

'But Mrs Sorrento told me she'd no money. Her husband had left her destitute...'

'I think she misled you there, Mr Kemp,' murmured Elvira, 'and in other ways as well. The children's names, for instance. It's just Luke, not a younger version of Luciano, and the little girl is Mary. They were told not to open their mouths.' Elvira giggled. 'Of course Luke opened his to drink your bottle of red ink. That's when I knew I'd got the right little boy... When I spoke to Annie Mungo first she said she didn't know what I was talking about, it wasn't her kids that went with Mrs Sorrento, but when I told her I'd seen the mole on Luke's back when I washed him, and seen it again when he had his shirt off at the playground that Saturday... Well, that's when she knew the game was up, and told me the whole story.' Elvira stopped, then continued with some hesitation. 'I did promise her, Mr Kemp, that she'd not get into any trouble. I mean, it's hardly a crime to let your children go out with another woman.'

'But why should Mrs Sorrento borrow someone else's children? I can't make head or tail of it. How well did this Mrs Mungo know our Mrs Sorrento?'

'She's seen her around the site, but not really to speak to. They lived at different ends. I did ask her to describe her, though, and it sounded the same person as came in to us.'

'You have been thorough. You really take my breath away, Elvira. I agree with you, the whole thing is very odd. I think I ought to do a little checking-up on Mrs Sorrento.'

'That's just what I wanted you to do. But it might be difficult. There's no doubt at all that she's really back in Sicily. I spoke to some of her nearer neighbours, and they all say the same thing. She left just after the inquest, and the caravan's been let to other people.'

Elvira got to her feet. 'Thanks for the drink, Mr Kemp—and for listening. Quite like old times, it's been.' She gave another giggle. 'I'd better go to the loo on the way out, even we plebs have to do that! I'm not used to so much sherry...'

As she was going out, she suddenly stopped. 'I've got it! Her knocking into me and me having to pick up all the papers, there was something else at the time surprised me, and then went right out of my head. Mr Kemp, did you tell her which door it was?'

'Who are we talking about now? Oh, Mrs Proby... I only told her the ladies' room was at the end of the corridor. After all, it is marked.'

'Not today it isn't. We've got the decorators in, remember? There are three doors at the end of that corridor, all kept closed, and none of them has any lettering on them just now. Yet she walked straight into the right one first time. Even in the rush she was in she never hesitated. At the speed she was going she could have knocked herself out on that steel shelf that sticks out in the stationery cupboard, or she could have ended up in the gents...'

In her excitement, Elvira was gabbling. I shouldn't have given her that second sherry, thought Kemp.

'Come on, super sleuth,' he said briskly, as he locked up his desk. 'I'd better run you home before your husband suspects we're having an office romance.'

'Some hope,' she told him with a return of her earlier asperity, 'specially now that you've got your eye on higher things...'

NINE

Kemp ran his fingers over the deckle-edge as if testing for psychic guidance before replacing the card on the mantelpiece beside the clock given to his father on retirement. It looked just as out of place there as it had done when propped up on his office desk but at least it was safe from Elvira's withering glances.

'Of course you must still come with us,' Lettice had exclaimed when he told her he was doubtful of his welcome after the Courtenays' strange behaviour. 'The twins are always doing things like that. Taking people up one minute, freezing them out the next. They find it amusing, but it doesn't mean a thing. It'll be all forgotten when they see you again.'

'I don't like being taken up, as you put it,' Kemp had said stubbornly. 'I'm not a piece of basketwork. Anyway, I can't see where I went wrong with them. Their business was put through promptly, and they'd no complaints on that score. I did offer them some advice on planning, but I was as polite as any lawyer can be when he knows it's falling on deaf ears.'

'Then that's all right, then.' Lettice's voice on the phone had been cheerful. 'It's only Vivian who's got bees in his bonnet about pop festivals, you can hear them buzzing in our department... But you must have made a hit with Venetia, Lennox.'

'Why do you say that?' Kemp had asked cautiously.

'She's asked me for your private phone number. Oh, I know what you always say, that you only give it to your friends, but...'

'She wheedled it out of you?'

'Something like that. I didn't really think you'd mind. After all, the Courtenays are now very influential, they could bring you in a lot of business. I didn't think it would do any harm. She was so eager to have it...' Lettice's voice was trailing off. All Kemp could do was assure her that, no, he didn't mind, although he couldn't imagine why Venetia would want it—he had a perfectly good office telephone.

But of course it wasn't at the office that Venetia rang him.

'Lennox Kemp?' she said, 'what are you doing?'

'I'm holding the phone in one hand, and a glass of Beaujolais in the other. I'm sitting on a Parker-Knoll chair and the radio's playing Dvorak's Fifth. They're in the middle of the slow movement, and it's raining outside.'

Her laughter was very light, and tinkled above the music.

'Don't turn it down,' she said.

'I've no intention of turning it down. I like the New World.'

'I prefer the old one. Is your Beaujolais new, too?'

'I don't think so. I never could remember dates.'

'You seem to have forgotten ours. We have had no reply from you to our invitation.' He could almost see her pretty pout. Then she began singing, softly:

'Remember, remember, the Fifth of November,
With gunpowder, treason and plot . . .'

'Wasn't that when some poor fool tried to blow up Parliament?' said Kemp, responding to her mood.

'Only the House of Lords,' she corrected him, and he had to give her full marks for historical accuracy.

'I do remember that he came to a sticky end after they'd, quite literally I'm afraid, screwed the whole conspiracy out of him. Your Courtenay ancestors lived in brutal times, Mrs Proby. I trust they're not to be re-enacted at your masquerade?'

'What super fun if they could be! Vivian would enjoy racking a few planning officials. But with you, Lennox, we would be very gentle.'

'I refuse to put on motley.'

'You see yourself as a clown?' This was accompanied by so warm a chuckle that he could not take offence. Then, in a voice which put on sweet seriousness like honey, she went on: 'But we see you as a counsellor most grave and good . . .'

'If you're trying to quote *Hamlet*, it was a counsellor most still, most secret and most grave because by then he was dead as a doornail.'

'*Touché*, Lennox. I do admire a mind that can follow through. But you will come, won't you, if only to cast a cold eye on our revels?'

Kemp was beginning to feel the Courtenay effect again; it was rather pleasant being playfully seduced—at a safe distance. As the conversational game went on for some time it was as if the telephone line had become a high wire on which they were both showing off their verbal skills, as tightrope walkers might their fancy footwork. One slip of the tongue and down you go.

Only after he had said, eventually, 'Of course I shall come,' and with a little sighing noise she had put down the phone, did he realize how effectively he had been captured.

There was no way now he could not go. He took the invitation card from the mantelpiece and wrote a formal acceptance as the last bars of the symphony faded into silence. Damn it, he thought, she made me miss it.

By the next morning he was glad he had at least resolved that problem, there were plenty of others on his desk to tackle and, calling to mind Elvira's strictures, one of these was foremost.

He rang the Newtown Police Station, and was lucky to catch Detective-Inspector Upshire before he left.

'Mrs Sorrento? Of course she went off to Sicily right after the inquest. No, it wasn't for a holiday, she said she wouldn't be coming back... No, she hasn't, my people would have known... What do you mean, did I see the children? She was hardly likely to bring them to the court, she left them with their grandmother, which was sensible. The WPC? Hang on, I'll ask her...'

Kemp spoke to WPC Prentiss himself.

'When you were at the caravan, Miss Prentiss, did you see the two Sorrento children?'

'They were asleep, Mr Kemp, in the back. There are two small bedrooms. I went into one with Mrs Sorrento to get some face tissues because she'd been crying... No, of course we didn't wake the children, poor little souls. Mrs Sorrento said they wouldn't understand anyway about their father... She was distressed herself, as who wouldn't be? I stayed for a while, made her some tea, that kind of thing... But she said she'd be OK, she had good neighbours if she needed them. She told me she'd take the kids to her mother's in the morning. When I went back with Inspector Upshire the day of the inquest Mrs Sorrento said her mother was looking after them... Where? I've no idea ... Some place in Camden Town I think... She told me that's where she'd come from originally before she got a job in one of the brush factories out here.'

'Thank you, Miss Prentiss. What do you think of Julie Sorrento, yourself?'

'She was upset of course but not grief-stricken, if you know what I mean. A bit limited, I suppose. She wasn't very bright, but quite tough like most of these

East End girls. I really don't know what you want me to say, Mr Kemp.'

'Only your own impression of her. You've had experience of such sad occasions.'

'I'm afraid I have. Julie Sorrento was no different from the others. When you have to break news of fatal accidents you do get to know the reactions. Some are really distraught, even hysterical. Julie Sorrento wasn't like that... I think she took in what had happened, but she'd already been convinced that he'd deserted her and the kids so she wasn't totally unprepared. I'm afraid that's about all I can tell you.'

Kemp used the lunch-hour to go out to The Willows. The Council had done a good job on the old gipsy encampment, the caravans were arranged in an orderly fashion with decent space around each. No. 32, which had housed the Sorrentos, even had a tiny plot of flowers now sadly in decay. It was tucked into a corner of the site and almost hidden behind hawthorn hedges which must have been planted some time ago, possibly to give a measure of privacy to the little home.

No use disturbing the newcomers, so he knocked on the nearest door which was No. 34, but there was no reply. Coming back through the broken picket fence, he heard a shout.

'They ain't in... You lookin' for the Smiths?'

An ample, middle-aged woman was watching him from the door of No. 33. Kemp walked over to her.

Hers was a tidy place, cheerful red-checked curtains at the windows, geraniums still scarlet in pots beside the path. He leaned over her gate as she came down to him, pleased to have some conversation.

'Both workin' folk, the Smiths. Never in day-times. You sellin' summat?'

'No, I'm not. As a matter of fact I just wanted to see where the Sorrento family had lived. I was Mrs Sorrento's solicitor.'

Mrs Carter, as she told him her name was, seemed quite satisfied by this vague explanation. Kemp could only think that she knew little of lawyers and considered any activity of theirs to be outside her comprehension. 'Oh, them,' she said, glancing over at No. 32. 'They've gone away.'

'So I understand. Were you a friend of theirs?'

'No ways. Him I'd see out in the garden. Liked his garden, did Mr Sorrento. Like a bit of peace, more like. She'd a tongue on her, that one. Short in the legs and long in the mouth.'

'But you didn't know Mrs Sorrento well?'

'Scarcely passed the time o' day with her. Not my sort.' Mrs Carter gave a sniff. She had pleasant, homely features folded in fat, and gray hair pushed up under a woollen scarf. 'Don't get me wrong, there's all kinds on this site. Me and my hubby came here when he retired, and when he passed on I just stayed. It's quiet enough in the day. Most's at work, kids at school ... Suits me.'

'The Sorrentos have two children?'

'That's right. Lukey and Maria. Never bothered me, I'll say that for Mrs Sorrento—but mebbe it was him saw to that. They'd play quiet-like round the garden, and I'd see her take them down the shops, but their caravan bein' in the corner they never disturbed no one. Sad, what happened to Mr Sorrento, though ... I'm not talkin' out of turn, I hope. What did you say your name was?'

'Kemp. Lennox Kemp.'

'Well, she was sluttish in her ways, Mr Kemp. Never made him a decent meal that I could see. Passed here with her bags full of that there convenience food. And him such a hard worker, too. Drove him to the drink with her moanin'. Allus wantin' summat new. And the tatty clothes on her, and never washed...' Mrs Carter caught Kemp's eye, and bridled. 'I sees her washin' line from my back window. Allus know what a wife's like by her clothes-line, that's what I say.'

'Mrs Sorrento said she had good neighbours ... when she lost her husband, I mean.'

Mrs Carter stared.

'That ain't so. There's no one here knew her at all. See for yourself, Mr Kemp.' She waved a podgy hand round this deserted corner of the site and he saw what she meant. None of the dwellings were anywhere near No. 32 except for No. 34 and Mrs Carter's own.

'The Smiths, they was on holiday the night they come and told her, them over there was new in that week, and she never came askin' for any help from me. Not that I wouldn't have rallied round, in the circumstances, like, but she never came to my door. I seen the police car myself and all the hubbub but 'twasn't my place to go interferin'... Not like as if we'd been friends. I only hears about it at the shops next day.'

'Well, Mrs Sorrento had her mother to go to, I suppose.'

Mrs Carter nodded.

'That's what's said. She lives Camden Town ways... Always runnin' off there, she was, with the kids. I don't hold with all that goin' home to your ma if things gets rough. I says if you made your marriage bed that's how you got to lie in it. She shouldn't have got married in the first place, and him a Catholic, too.'

'It takes all sorts, Mrs Carter,' said Kemp cheerfully, dropping his own gem of homespun philosophy.

'Hope I've not spoken ill...' As one who lived alone, Mrs Carter's tongue was apt to run on by itself, and she was aware of it. 'I'm right sorry for the girl, really, losin' her man like that. It's a good thing his family's lookin' after her and the kids, least that's what's said... I'll say that for the Eyeties, they take care of their own.'

'She's really gone to Sicily, then?'

'Oh, she's there all right. I heard that down at the shops. One of the younger ones, t'other end of site,

she had a postcard. Her lad used to play with
Lukey... Naw, Mr Kemp, I can't help you there.
One-parent families they call 'em. Ain't any of my
business, but...'

To forestall another burst of moral sentiments,
Kemp thanked her hastily, and went on his way.

That would be his next call; Annie Mungo of the
rent-a-child agency. Yet, as he walked through the
ranks of silent caravans only occasionally hearing
the sound of a crying baby, the clatter of dishes, the
muffled grinding of washing-machines, past the little groups of women trailing shopping-bags, or the
solitary ones standing in their doors just staring
out—so little animation, simply those small signs of
other lives—he guessed existence here was no joking
matter. In desperation the Council had housed them,
and in desperation they had accepted what was offered because there was nowhere else. Even in Newtown the building of Council houses had been
stopped, the neat rows of red-brick dwellings had
absorbed those who had come first, the others must
fend for themselves or, if homeless for whatever
reason, a distracted Council would provide this, the
shelter of the caravans—the very word invoked a
feeling of transience, an in-between land, a temporary stopping-place... The Sorrentos had been here
for years; no wonder Julie had grown into the hope-
less sloven he'd seen—and inwardly despised.

It was a bleak day, the weather presaging winter, not a day for playing in the park. He hoped Mrs Mungo would be at home.

He had to ask around before he found her caravan, but at last someone pointed it out to him. 'Last one on the line, that's Mrs Mungo's, and she's home. I seen her go in half an hour ago...'

It was cleaner and tidier than some of the others. An effort had been made to brighten up the paintwork, there was a swing and a battered seesaw within the little plot.

Kemp knocked, and heard children's voices inside. When the door opened, the woman had the child he had known as Maria clutching at her skirt.

'Mrs Mungo?'

'Yes?' she inquired cautiously. She was in her late twenties, reddish-fair with freckles on a pale skin, and a mouth that knew how to smile, though it wasn't smiling now. 'You're not from the DHSS?'

'I should hope not,' said Kemp with enough emphasis to put humour into the words. 'Have they been bothering you?'

'When have they not...' There was relief in her china-blue eyes, but wariness remained. 'What can I do for you, then?'

It was easier than Kemp had imagined but only because Elvira had paved the way. When he had explained who he was, Annie Mungo said: 'Well, you'd best come in, Mr Kemp. I've not done anything wrong that I can see.'

Kemp patted the curly head of the little girl, who looked up at him trustingly as she had done before.

'Hello, Mary,' he said as he followed Mrs Mungo into the living-room which was surprisingly spacious and well-ordered. At a table by the window the boy, Luke, was playing with alphabet blocks and there were rows of toys arranged on shelves above his head.

'They're yours, Mary and Luke?'

''Course they are. And born legitimate if it's any business of yours. I divorced their dad years ago. Mungo's my maiden name.'

She had an accent—Scottish or Irish? She soon let him know. She was from Glasgow originally, and, unlike Julie Sorrento, she was bright and easy to talk to. Having allayed her initial nervousness, Kemp found her both frank and perceptive.

'I can see why you've come,' she said as she made tea for them both. 'It did strike me as odd when Mrs Sorrento arrived at my door that day last August and asked if she could take the children out.'

'How well did you know her?'

'I didn't know her at all. It was him I used to see at the playground on Saturdays. He used to take them with him to his allotment, he told me, but he lost that so he brought them to the park. We got talking about what a coincidence it was our kids having nearly the same names, and Italian fathers... It was quite a joke between us. He was a nice person, Mr Sorrento, quiet and had nice manners, even though his English was limited.'

'But you didn't know his wife?'

'I'd seen her around the site, of course, and down at the shops. I knew who she was, but she wasn't a friend of mine.'

Annie Mungo put the tray of tea on the flap below the serving-hatch, fetched orange juice for the children, and sat down.

'Perhaps I oughtn't to say this, but I thought Mrs Sorrento was a bit of a trollop. She only dressed properly when she was off somewhere, and she never saw to the kids' clothes. That hair of hers! She had an afro, then she dyed it purple, then she went all black and Rastafarian...'

'What did she say to you the day she came?'

'That her husband had gone off and left her, that she had to go down to the Social Services, and see a lawyer about getting maintenance. She was all there when it came to that... And I should know, I've been through it myself.'

'Why'd she want to take your children?'

Annie shrugged. 'Said hers were at their gran's— and she didn't want her to know Luciano had left her. But I could see her point about wanting to have kids with her. I bet you've never had to go to the DHSS in Newtown... You can get shoved around for hours, but if you've got children with you, it does help. She made sense there... It would be the only

way to get a bit of action out of our Mrs Wigram.
You know Mrs Wigram?'

'Only by the sound of her voice.'

'Then you know her,' said Annie firmly. 'Mrs
Wigram's got a heart of stone, but if there's one
thing she can't stand it's a crying bairn. It wouldn't
make her any more sympathetic to your claim but
she'd be so irritated with herself you'd get what you
wanted—and a damn sight quicker. Julie Sorrento
said she'd heard that said around the site, and, well,
I told her it was true... Anyway, I didn't mind her
having the kids for an afternoon, there was no harm
in it, I did know her husband, after all. There was
nothing sinister about it, Mr Kemp. Of course, afterwards, when I heard what had happened to him,
I was so shocked...'

'You had liked him?'

'Mr Kemp, I know a good Italian husband when I
see one. And I should know... I married a wrong
'un. "Lucky" they tell me Mr Sorrento was called.
I'd have said she was the lucky one... But he was
depressed. He got so frustrated about that allotment of his. He liked growing things, should have
been a farmer, I guess. He told me once that if he
could only get a bit of land back there in Sicily, he'd
go like a shot and take the whole family. Sad, when
you come to think of it...'

She poured out more tea. She has seen hard times
herself, thought Kemp, but she has a kind nature and
a lot of courage. Her children were well cared for; she

was doing her best for them. He hated what he had to ask next.

'She offered you something?' he said gently.

Annie's face reddened, and she hesitated before she spoke.

'She brought some toys—they were far more expensive than I could ever afford. She said Luciano was always buying too many... But, to be honest, Mr Kemp, it was when she brought the children back and insisted on giving me ten pounds that I felt...' She put a hand up to her mouth. 'Well, I don't know what I felt, really. Julie Sorrento said she'd money from some lottery or other she didn't want the DHSS knowing about...and there would be more if I never told anyone about her borrowing the children.' It was all coming out now in a rush. 'There was an envelope pushed through my door with twenty pounds in it. That would be after the inquest... I did begin to wonder, then. But I thought to myself—well, we all try to keep things from them at the Social Services. We have to, Mr Kemp, it's the only way we can keep our end up... So that's what I thought when your secretary came, that they'd found out about the money I'd had...'

Kemp could see how it could have been, but if he had come to Annie Mungo expecting some sinister development, he had to admit to disappointment. Her story hung together so far as she was able to tell it although he could see holes that he could not fill in with any sensible material. She had been honest with him, if not to the welfare services, but he reckoned that was an on-going battle and one in which he had no wish to take sides.

Luke had come over for biscuits. 'I seen you,' he said, raising dark smiling eyes. 'I ate your ink...'

Annie Mungo burst out laughing, releasing the tension in her. 'Your girl told me. I couldn't make head or tail of it when Mrs Sorrento brought the children back. Luke kept on about all the red stuff and having his face washed...'

'Didn't Mrs Sorrento explain?'

'She never stopped more than a minute. She thrust that money at me, told me there would be more where that came from, and then rushed off again. I never saw her after that.'

'What, not even on the caravan site?'

Annie shook her head. 'People said she'd gone to her mother's. And now she's in Sicily. She's even sent me a card.'

'May I see it?'

'I've no idea where it's gone.' Annie got up and began rummaging in a little desk set into a corner. 'Luke, that nice picture that came, the one with the blue sky and the mountain...?'

'All cut up...' He ran over to his table and came back with a pair of child's scissors. Annie gave a sigh. 'Sorry,' she said with a grin, 'Luke's into cutting out scraps from magazines and things. And it's days ago since the card came. I'd have cleared up all the bits by now—you can't keep anything in a place this size. Anyway, all it said was that they were all settled, the sun was shining, thanks again, love, Julie.'

Luke had clambered up on a chair and was pulling stuff about on his shelf. He got what he wanted and came down. 'Pretty 'tamp...' he said, holding it out on the end of his finger.

Kemp took it. It was a torn-off stamp, and it had been properly cancelled with a Sicilian postmark.

'Well, that seems to be that,' he said, getting to his feet, 'I'm sorry I've had to bother you, Mrs Mungo, and thanks for being so frank with me.'

'You won't tell them about the money?'

'Tell the formidable Mrs Wigram? Not bloody likely.'

'It's just that I can't stand them making inquiries. You know how it is...' Something in Kemp's manner, perhaps a subtle intimation she had that, in the struggle to live according to their natures, they might well be on the same side, made her confide in him. 'I do odd jobs, you see, cleaning at people's houses where they don't mind me taking the children. They pay cash, and that comes in useful...'

And never gets declared when drawing welfare benefits... Well, he supposed, it was no worse than deliberate tax evasion, or even the elaborate tax avoidance schemes he set up for clients who had heaped up riches and grudged the State its proper portion.

'My dear Annie,' he said, putting up a hand, 'I cannot be seen to condone. Just take it that I'd rather not know...'

'I'm only telling you this because you're so interested in Julie Sorrento. That was the first time I saw her away from the site...' She stopped.

'Go on. You're quite right, I am still interested in her.'

'Well, it was some time back in July I was told they wanted waitresses at the Golden Slipper. You know, the club place?'

Kemp nodded. Newtown's one and only nightspot.

'One of my girlfriends here worked at the Club but she wanted a weekend off, and she asked me to take her place. I've got a nice neighbour who'll mind the children in the evenings if I don't do it too often... Anyway, the money was good. It was there I saw the Sorrentos. He had a brother over from Sicily and they were celebrating with a supper party. Mrs Sorrento looked like she always did, mini-skirt up to here and plunging neckline down to you know where. I know because I was serving their table. But it was the company they were in that really surprised me. Real high society... the folks that live on the hill...'

'Who do you mean?'

'Why, those Courtenays from the Manor. You must surely have heard of the Courtenays, Mr Kemp?'

TEN

KEMP WAS STUMPED. He admitted as much to Elvira, who was sympathetic because she felt guilty of stepping out of line. 'I'm sorry,' she said lamely, as she gathered up files and tapes, 'I didn't mean you had to go out there and see these people...'

'And get precisely nowhere. Which made me come back and get through a rare load of work from sheer frustration. Now I want to think.'

'It all sounds, well, quite sensible,' Elvira said pensively, on her way to the door, 'but silly at the same time. To go to all that trouble just to have two kids with you when you go for welfare...'

'It's because it sounds so silly that it may very well be true. None of us knows how the other half lives... There, I'm talking in comfortable clichés like Mrs Carter.'

'You really think there's nothing in it, then? It all happened just like that?'

'You sound disappointed, Elvira. You thought you were on the trail of some deep mysterious conspiracy, and all we find are a couple of incompetents trying to cheat the system.'

Elvira's mouth had opened to say something else, but hearing the acerbic note in his voice, she shut it tight, and departed quietly; when Mr Kemp was in this mood he was better left to do his own thinking.

Kemp looked gloomily at the scribbled notes he'd taken on his first interview with Julie Sorrento but they didn't tell him much now except that there'd been a few lies. They were small lies, and with someone of her mental calibre and incoherence they were probably inevitable. There he was again, putting her down! Yet from those he'd talked to who had any acquaintance with her, from John Upshire to Mrs Carter, she had appeared to them as she had appeared to him: an inadequate wife, an indifferent mother, keen on new clothes and make-up but without either the means or the know-how to look other than—what was that word Annie had used?—grotty. Grotty just about summed up poor Julie, even to the suggestion of stubborn grit when it came down to money and her matrimonial rights.

He pulled the phone towards him and dialled. Yes, WPC Prentiss was in the station.

'I'm being a nuisance again, Miss Prentiss. About Mrs Sorrento... Did anyone have the address of her mother in Camden Town?'

'I'll have to look out the file, Mr Kemp. It's been put away.' There was a pointed rebuke in her voice. 'I'll have to ring you back.'

Waiting for her call, Kemp whirled his chair round and looked out of the window. Dusk was closing in early on the rooftops. October had gone out like a light, and the start of November had brought freezing temperatures and a dank fog that clung about the old valley of the Lea River where Newtown had been built. The streets were full of youngsters displaying stuffed grotesques and hopeful money-boxes, every waste patch had its pile of rubbish cut and dried ready for the bonfires. Really, that man, Guy Fawkes, had a lot to answer for three hundred and eighty years on...

There was a great uneasiness growing in Kemp's mind. He had kept back one thing from Elvira: that supper-party at the Golden Slipper Club, the Sorrentos in the company of the Courtenays. Why hadn't he told her? Was it simply that she might have sniffed and said: 'Oh, you and your obsession with those people!' Or was it that the coincidence was still too strange, too disturbing, and he himself had not yet taken it in? It meant nothing. The Courtenays got about, the Club was the only one of its kind in Newtown... Yet they had been at the same table. He would have expected the twins' playground to have been the West End... Perhaps, of course, they were 'slumming'—that would be in their character. But it had happened in July, according to Mrs Mungo, which tied in with Alfredo Sorrento's visit. Silas Courtenay had died in July, presumably Vivian and Venetia were up for the funeral and they too were celebrating...

The phone rang, and he picked it up.

WPC Prentiss was not pleased with him. 'We never had a note of the mother's address,' she told him. 'There wasn't any need. It was only where she'd taken the children, she herself was always available at the caravan. I don't know what you're making all this fuss for, Mr Kemp. Everything was properly done. Nobody wanted to harass Mrs Sorrento. I was with her on both occasions, and I can tell you that despite her distress she was all right... I mean, she wasn't suicidal or anything. And she was offered counselling and that kind of thing. Really, I don't see what more we could have done...' She was running out of words, and getting more rattled every minute. 'I've had to tell the Inspector why I was looking out that file... He doesn't like us to waste our time, you know.'

Kemp smoothed her ruffled feathers with fulsome words of thanks and she rang off, not totally mollified.

A waste of time. And that's exactly what it had been, Kemp thought moodily. He had only gone out there to The Willows because of what Elvira had hinted at, he had felt the sting of her contempt at his preoccupation with Venetia Courtenay while neglecting other matters. He suddenly remembered how his conscience had pricked him when John Upshire told him about the death of Julie Sorrento's husband... he knew in his bones that he had somehow failed in duty to his client.

He had the same feeling now. At the back of his mind there was a nagging doubt, almost as if he had arrived in court confident of his preparation in a case only to find he had forgotten one crucial piece of evidence. Every lawyer's nightmare, he told himself ruefully; it's an occupational hazard. But this wasn't a case. All he had been presented with was a string of trivial data which simply would not add up. It was as though he had a psychological block which prevented him from bringing reason to bear directly upon the problem. Yet there was no problem, just this sensation that there was something left unfinished, something overlooked, something wrong...

He had always been conscious that there were two warring elements in his nature, one the special rational side which fed on facts, tangible proofs, incontrovertible premises on which he could build slowly and meticulously to reach an apt conclusion; the other, the wayward side was pure instinct, less soundly based but still a force that could set alarm bells ringing if he would only listen. It was instinct which was trying to lead him now, giving him a warning that things he had seen as superficial had a deeper significance, that somewhere there was a danger he had not recognized.

He moved restlessly, frowning in concentration... It came almost as a relief when Elvira knocked on his door.

'Mrs Francis is here to pay her account. Can you spare her a minute?'

Kemp jumped to his feet. 'Of course. Show her in.'

Amy was in fine fettle, as she herself would have described it. She brought a breath of outside air into his stuffy office.

'I've settled with your cashier, but I just wanted to say a word of thanks.'

'No need for that. But do sit down. I've not seen you for a while but I hear the new business is going well. How is Mrs Courtenay?'

'Better than she's been for years. She's got a job to do and she's revelling in it. A much maligned lady, Blanche. A bit late perhaps to come out of her shell but...'

'Why'd she need a shell in the first place?'

'Should I be gossiping, Lennox?'

'Feel free. I was just thinking I'd lost my talent in that direction. Comes of being a respectable solicitor instead of an investigating agent.'

'You said that almost with regret.' Amy Francis was amused. 'I think you rather enjoyed the seamy side.'

'Enjoyed isn't the right word... The pay was nothing like so good. But it did give me an instinct.' Now why had he used that word?

'An instinct for people?' said Amy shrewdly. 'Well, don't shout it in the streets or you'll frighten the horses. You seem very interested in the Courtenays?'

Kemp spread his hands. 'They're a new breed of planet swum into my ken...'

Amy considered. She believed in plain speaking, and she trusted Kemp.

'My knowledge is confined to Blanche, and that merely in the last few years. What I know of her I like, but of course there are hidden areas about which I can only surmise.'

'She was widowed young. She must have been distressed.'

'Distressed? Come off it ... It's the lower orders that get distressed and Blanche was never one of those. Besides, Charles Courtenay and she were children of their time and class, they did what their families expected of them. It was an arranged marriage from the start, so his loss to her was purely financial. She became, if you like, a distressed gentlewoman.'

Kemp saw her point.

'Poverty is relative. Blanche thought herself badly done by?'

'In her view, yes. She had to cut her charge account at Harrods, and she couldn't buy the strings of horses she wanted, so she slid off into her own world of good-looking grooms and dodgy trainers. That didn't please Silas, so he kept her short. He disliked the hunting and racing scene as much as he did the theatre.'

'Which explains why he wouldn't support Venetia's bid for an acting career?'

'You know about that? And he didn't take kindly to Vivian's scheme to tour the country with a rock group. Oh yes, Vivian had great plans to outdo the Rolling Stones.'

'Two very frustrated young people with potential for good or evil. They would naturally cleave to one another, and they ended up... warped.'

Amy's bright eyes clouded over.

'That's crude, Lennox. But as you've said it, I'm afraid it's true. Blanche hoped... when Venetia got married, it would stop but it didn't. I'm sorry for Lewis Proby even though I don't really like him much. He's creepy, and everyone knows he only married her for her expectations. He lost out on that, too. He had his father's stockbroking firm once but it went under years ago and now he's only an employee.'

'The waiting years have taken their toll,' Kemp remarked, a trifle sententiously, 'and now that the hoped-for wealth has come neither of the twins seems to me wildly happy...'

'You've noticed it, too? I thought I was imagining things... When I've met them recently they struck me as more insecure than ever, as if they were living on the edge of a precipice.'

Kemp was surprised; it was unlike Amy Francis to invoke such a metaphor, the impression must have been strong in her mind.

'I'm glad I've rescued Blanche,' she went on, more cheerfully. 'Venetia had been bothering her, I don't know why. For years now the twins ignored their mother, then Venetia keeps on at her reviving old memories . . .'

'What about?'

'Their father, mostly. Wanted to know what he was like, all about him. Now, that might have been perfectly natural at twenty—in fact Blanche would have been pleased if they'd shown any interest when they were younger—but in a woman of thirty-five, which is what Venetia is, it seemed a bit odd to Blanche. Which reminds me, I've left Blanche in charge . . . I must get back to her.'

She got to her feet.

'By the way, Lennox, are you going to this monstrous charade of theirs tomorrow night? They seem to have asked everybody.'

Kemp laughed. 'Thanks for putting it that way. Yes, I was asked, and yes, I'll probably go. Will you be there?'

'Not my thing at all, but I can't let Blanche down. We're taking that nice Mrs Beresford from the Library. She didn't want to go alone.'

'Has she found her young American?'

Amy stared. 'Why, did she lose him?'

'Oh, just a stray, came asking about footpaths round Ember, she got interested in him but he never came back.'

'Well, I've not seen any lost Americans lately— he'd have to be pretty dim if he got lost in Ember . . . We shall look forward, then, to seeing you tomorrow night. If we recognize you, that is . . .'

'You will. No fancy get-ups for me. They must take me as I am. What about you three ladies?'

Amy giggled self-consciously. 'You'll never believe this but we will be Mary, Queen of Scots and her attendants. Blanche's idea—she says the Elizabethan wing is to be opened up for the occasion.'

'The one Silas had restored?'

'Well, partly. All I know is that it will be bloody cold. There's no heating.'

'Isn't that where there's a secret room?'

'Who told you that? Lettice Warrender, I suppose. Blanche says it's only where they kept some French prisoner one of the Courtenays had captured in the time of Henry the Eighth.'

'When he was young and sportive and waged his wars in France. Henry in his youth was no slouch when it came to fighting, and neither were his courtiers when it came to raising money. French prisoners of high degree were ransomed for a goodly sum.'

'What a lot you know! I didn't think the story was true. Anyway, they're supposed to have kept the French nobleman in that room in conditions worthy of his status—except of course that he couldn't get out.'

'Until his price was paid by his relatives. A very civilized way of treating prisoners-of-war, and not one, I'm afraid, meted out to the common lot.'

'I think the chip on your shoulder ought to be hidden when you're up at the Manor,' said Amy with a laugh, as she went out, 'or the Courtenays might throw you in the dungeon.'

When she had gone, Kemp took up the telephone. His train of thought had not been interrupted to any great extent by her visit. There was one thing he had forgotten to do.

'Elvira? Can you get through to the DHSS office in Camden Town for me? Try to put the Supervisor on.'

The voice that eventually spoke was warmer and more helpful than Mrs Wigram's had been. No, he was informed, they did not have a Mrs Julie Sorrento on their books, and no claim for benefit had been made in her name.

Kemp sat back, and thought about it. Perhaps Julie Sorrento had decided to rely on private enterprise as enjoined by an unbenevolent Government and live for a time on the lottery money she'd said was all gone . . .

The phone rang. A sharp, angry voice at the other end said:

'John Upshire here. Where the hell have you been? I've been trying to get through to you.'

'I had a client, and I've been making some phone calls—'

'Too damn right you have. WPC Prentiss told me. What are you up to about Mrs Sorrento?'

'Nothing to put you in such a fizz. What's the matter?'

'Mrs Sorrento's the matter.' Kemp could hear the Inspector drawing a deep breath. 'I know you, Lennox, when you've got a bee in your bonnet about something. You're a stirrer. Made me wonder...so I thought it was high time I did a bit of checking myself. And what do I find?'

'Go on. You're dying to tell me.'

'Mrs Julie Sorrento never went on a flight to Sicily after the inquest. I've been on to the airlines, and there's no record of her at that date or since. Damn the woman! After she'd told me it was all arranged, said she'd the tickets booked for her and the kids...'

'Mrs Sorrento said a lot of things, John. Perhaps it's time you and I had a little talk about some of them.'

ELEVEN

FRIDAY, NOVEMBER 5, was a murky day with over-hanging cloud and the threat of rain, casting gloom among many expectant boys and girls. But by night-fall the skies had cleared; it would be dry and cold with perhaps a touch of frost later on. Mothers gave out woolly caps and scarves, warm gloves and words of admonition. Fathers checked the box of fireworks, tied rocket sticks to the palings and hoped that this year the blasted Catherine wheels would actually go round instead of just fizzing sadly on the fence.

By seven o'clock bonfires were glowing red like sudden blossoming roses all over the town. Bang and flash, swish and crackle, off went the rockets to expire in a brief shower of exploding stars, up and up in cascades of brilliant light went the little fountains, green, gold and crimson flared the tiny volcanoes, in and out of the darkness went the twinkling pinpoints of sparklers in the hands of happy children. On the outskirts, ever watchful, the fire-fighting services prowled around and around like the hosts of Midian, but Newtown held fast to safety and there were few accidents.

Everything was popping away merrily when Lennox Kemp climbed into John Ingray's car. 'Sensible man,' he remarked, 'you've not got dressed up either.'

'I've got my working clothes on,' said the veterinary surgeon, with a grin, 'right down to the boots. I'm going as a James Heriot character—the good-looking one. Anyway, I'm on call and I don't fancy attending a sick cow in doublet and hose just to keep up with that...' He jerked a thumb at the back seat where Lettice's dark head was lost in the billowing folds of her enormous sleeves. The great spread of her skirts took up the rest of the rear seating accommodation.

Kemp turned round. 'You look like a pincushion,' he said, admiringly, 'but I bet you're supposed to be Lady Lettice Knollys... Is that a stomacher you've got there?'

'If that's something to make your stomach ache, then that's what it is. It pinches in all the wrong places. But you're right, the last time I wore this dress was in a school pageant as Lady Lettice. That at least was summertime... I've got my warm undies on tonight. I know the Manor, those corridors will be freezing. You two will be all right.' She leaned forward to glance critically at their black roll-collar sweaters under heavy jackets. 'You look to me like a couple of burglars. I'll be surprised if they let you in.'

There was in fact surprisingly good organization at the gates of Courtenay Manor. Discreet gentlemen scrutinized invitation cards, waved on those who'd forgotten them once names and status had been established, and directed guests towards the various entertainments on offer. There were parking attendants and ushers, the latter got up as footmen in livery, period vaguely eighteenth-century, and serving girls in those costumes peculiar to roystering tavern scenes from old movies where the lacing is loose and the bodices scant, and bosoms overflow from both like wasted wine.

On the terrace where Silas Courtenay had sat among the roses counting his money, or the years he had left, the throng of people looked larger than the actual number because of the thickness and diversity of their dress. Padded plastic epaulettes rubbed shoulders with homespun monkish hoods, cardboard space helmets dodged highwaymen's hats, and cowboy boots scratched the silken shins of Persian maidens well-wrapped beneath their gauzy harem pants. This was no midsummer revel, everyone had an eye on the weather and doubts as to central heating within the mansion.

In spite of himself, Kemp found the scene quite pleasant. Money, of course, can buy anything including entrepreneurial skills, and he recalled Vivian's claim to have only the best. As an inaugural event this had all the makings of a successful debut for Courtenay Manor as a centre for high-class entertainment, or a venue for private parties, besides aiming a stab at the soft underbelly of the local planning establishment by introducing them to pop music of unimpeachable quality. The groups playing both inside and outside the Manor itself were good; Vivian had known exactly what he was doing.

This was confirmed when Mr Shenstone, Chief Planning Officer of the Development Corporation, clad in sombre evening dress but with a bright satin cummerbund and frilled shirt, bowed low to Lettice. He had obviously been sampling the hot punch which was sweet, strong, and very potent. 'My Lady Lettice—' he bent over her hand. 'May I have the honour?'

Lettice gave Kemp and John Ingray a pert backward glance as she latched herself on to the arm of her employer, and they both gravitated towards the music.

'Women's lib!' exclaimed John. 'I don't know why they bother...'

'Punch, Mr Ingray? It'll warm your boots...'

'Maisie?' John recognized his receptionist. 'What on earth are you doing here?'

'I'm a serving wench, an it please you, sir...'

Both men took a goblet. 'God help the animals tonight,' said John, 'this is jolly good stuff...'

Half of Newtown must be here, thought Kemp as he left John to exchange pleasantries with Maisie whose everyday starched white uniform had never given a hint as to the charms now so flagrantly displayed.

Kemp climbed the steps to the terrace and leant on the stone balustrade. Below him people were already dancing, rather self-consciously, on the lawn, kicking their heels up out of the damp grass just beginning to gather rime. The shimmer of whiteness made the dark figures ghostly as they cavorted in their outlandish trappings, but the steady beat of a rock band was getting to them—as were the liveried footmen with trays of drinks—so that as the music strengthened so their feet stomped harder, and their gyrations whirled ever faster and wilder.

Kemp felt the cold stone numbing his fingers so he crossed the terrace towards the opened garden doors which led, he supposed, into the green drawing-room. He found himself both anticipating and fearing his meeting with Venetia Courtenay. This was her proper setting, but with the thought came the knowledge that it was their setting, hers and Vivian's. This was what they had waited for, screwed their guts out for all those waiting years. This was their birthday celebration, the first since coming into their power, this was their night. He took another glass of punch—at least the grasp of it would thaw his fingertips. He was drawn towards the lighted windows and the sounds of voices inside. He was also hungry, and the supper banquet was to be served at ten.

Already, the mood had been set. Vivian's contacts in the record industry, about which he had boasted, had responded well. The heady mixture of hot jazz, nostalgic rock, the beat of heavy metal, even the sweet-and-sour lyrics of the day wailed into the controlled microphones all over the house and grounds could have left no withers unwrung... The insistent sound swung high out into the empty night and low around the courtyard walls, reviving memories in the old, palpitating hopes in the young. Kemp felt it himself, that awfully trashy significance which popular music has, threading his ears, stitching up his senses...

Briefly, as he entered the drawing-room, he glimpsed the twins circulating, each with their own attendant courtiers, or standing on either side of the great fireplace tonight filled with flaming logs.

In a gesture, defiant yet predictable, they wore identical costumes, black velvet with stark white lace at neck and cuff, black silk stockings and silver-buckled shoes, two Jacobean gentlemen out on the spree. It seemed a favourite period of theirs, Jacobean England, that dangerous edge after the Tudor effulgence when the playwrights were only mirroring the times with their dramas of lust, violence and murder, the incestuous undercurrents of a state breaking down as the century turned...

Venetia had sought Kemp's eyes across the room, and raised the black domino mask which covered hers. She waved to him but before he could reach her he was intercepted by a group of noble dames whose vast panniered skirts barred his way. There was no mistaking Blanche Courtenay. This was not the young Mary of France and Scotland that Clouet had painted but the stooped, rheumatic, middle-aged Queen of Fotheringay, only the distinctive pearl-edged cap giving her away—that and the white ruff, the long black dress and the scarlet petticoat.

'Your Majesty!' Kemp bowed low, and smiled.

'Isn't she splendid?' whispered Amy Francis. Indeed, they were all splendid: Amy herself, one of her stable girls, a surprising Paula Warrender, and Lydia Beresford.

'Let me see,' said Kemp, standing back to admire them. 'There's Mary Beaton, and Mary Seton, and Mary Carmichael...'

'And me...' exclaimed Lydia.

'Mary Hamilton... I'm afraid you're the one who comes to a bad end, Mrs Beresford. Unless your missing American rides to your rescue on a white charger.' The occasion seemed to demand some frivolous expression of gallantry, and Kemp entered into the spirit of it.

Lydia Beresford was delighted by his teasing. She was only drinking fruit juice but she raised her glass to him, her eyes sparkling. The stable-girl, whose name was Prue and who had obviously been co-opted to make up the numbers, giggled. 'Have you got an admirer, Mrs Beresford? What's all this about an American?'

Lydia launched into her tale while the others listened. It was all apparently new to them, and under the spell of the party atmosphere, she made the most of the telling.

'Oh, quite the most handsome man ... Italianate good looks, I think one would call them ...' Urged on by Prue, Lydia was being quite carried away by what was in fact only a vague memory, but small embellishments seemed to be the thing tonight when everyone was larger and stranger than life. 'And so quiet and charming for an American ...'

Kemp had sensed her standing behind him for some moments, a breath of her perfume, the soft touch of velvet brushing against the back of his head. He didn't turn round but he knew her before she spoke.

'How magnificent you all are ... Very regal, Mummy, and quite the proper dress for an execution. Only a joke, Lennox ...' Pretty mouth laughing beneath the mask. 'You, on the other hand, look as if you've come to steal the silver. Don't waste your time, the caterers are well insured. Ah, the brother of my heart ...'

Vivian had come up to stand beside her, a pale languid hand upon her sleeve. Blanche Courtenay gave them a look which was not queenly. There was an uncomfortable silence.

A gong boomed out, and Venetia clapped her hands.

'Ten o'clock. Time for feasting, then the fireworks ... Shall we lead the way, Mother dear?'

The Great Hall had been set out with two long tables lit by candles and extravagantly decorated with vine leaves and trailing ivy. There were silver-gilt bowls piled high with crystallized fruits, enamelled dishes of nuts and exotic sweetmeats, and fluted glass stands bearing miracles in pink-and-white spun sugar.

'Move that tower of candy-floss,' commanded Lettice who was seated opposite to Kemp. 'I want a word with you.' Kemp did as he was told and she leant across and whispered: 'You've seen fireworks before... When the time comes we'll slip away and I'll show you the Prisoner's Room.'

On taking stock, Kemp reckoned there were about a hundred guests present, and he could not fault the arrangements. The cutlery shone, the glasses were sparkling crystal, the plates fine porcelain, and the place-names nestled beside finger-bowls complete with floating petals of rose and geranium. It was all very glitzy, in the spirit of the 'eighties: if you have it, you display it; if you haven't, you fake it.

One person in the room was certainly not fooled. As they sat down he heard the high well-bred voice of Mrs Courtenay asking querulously: 'Where'd all this stuff come from? In my day, Silas used plain crocks...'

'The caterers, I suppose.' Paula Warrender's tone had been a put-down, yet she had fingered the white damask cloth with some envy. 'They supply it all— for a price. Londoners, of course...'

And thank God for that, thought Kemp, tasting his soup. He had only a hazy idea of what was actually eaten in either mediaeval or Tudor times but imagined it as pretty disgusting even in the highest circles, so he was pleased to see that the caterers had been willing to sacrifice history in the interests of the consumers' health. Somewhere an ox had been roasted, and there was the obligatory boar's head looking as surprised as any animal would when its mouth is stuffed with a large Bramley. All these dishes, along with fat capons, whole fish, and saucy little suckling pigs glazed to their eyeballs, were brought in with style, arranged on side-tables and expertly carved at each course. The vegetables, to everyone's relief, were modern.

The loud music had ceased—presumably the various musicians were being fed below stairs—but in a corner of the Great Hall a group played soft guitars, the sound a background rather than a disturbance to the diners. They had a girl singer with a nice feeling for folksongs, and at one point she sang The Four Maries:

'Yestreen the Queen had four Maries,
Tonight she'll hae but three . . .
There was Mary Beaton, and Mary Seton,
And Mary Carmichael, and me.'

People laughed across the room and raised their glasses to Blanche Courtenay and her entourage.

The singer's voice rose plaintively:

'Oh, little did my Mither ken
The day she cradled me,
The lands that I should travel over,
The death that I should dee...'

The note died away, and there was a burst of clapping. Even Blanche, who was not entirely at home, either with her skirts or with the party in general, looked for the moment pleased.

For the most part, however—as must have been the fate of Court musicians in the past—the folk-groups were ignored. The acoustics of the hall meant the higher notes disappeared up the wide staircase while the words stood no chance above the hubbub of the chattering classes at table.

Above the racket Kemp heard Vivian holding forth on the future possibilities of the Manor: 'A weekend in Elizabethan splendour at a thousand pounds a time... Shootin' and fishin' thrown in...'

I don't suppose I'll be given credit for that little money-spinner, Kemp reflected, and wondered whether a haunting might also be arranged. The French prisoner perhaps, although from what Kemp had read of the affair the relatives had paid up and the nobleman had been released in accordance with the mediaeval rules of the game. In the meantime Mr Shenstone of Planning looked shaken, but mightily impressed as if the notion that hundreds of well-heeled tourists might flock in to Newtown to do their shopping was something he would think about when he'd recovered from the effects of hot punch.

At the banquet itself the only drink, except for those who eschewed alcohol, was champagne, pink this time but none the worse for that. Kemp drank sparingly, listened to conversations around him, and paid courteous attention to his lady companions on either side, neither of whom were known to him. Venetia was at the head of his table, flanked by her husband on one hand, and Arnold Crayshaw on the other. Lewis Proby looked positively melancholic in his dark grey pinstripes—Kemp wondered if he wore striped pyjamas in bed—but Arnold Crayshaw seemed to have got himself up in some kind of Dickensian gear and was having trouble negotiating his glass over his high satin stock. To Kemp's watchful eye, Venetia herself appeared rather subdued but perhaps that was only the effect on her of these two companions, the one too jovial, the other as downcast as a seller in a falling market. When her voice did ring out it had a strident note, and although from time to time her wit drew laughter from that end of the table her own was forced as if her heart was not in the performance, nor her mind on jesting.

As head of the other table Vivian was in blatant form, relishing praise from sycophants around him, and unblushingly taking all the credit for the evening's enterprise. Well, good luck to him, thought

Kemp, perhaps something might yet be made of him . . .

Toasts were drunk. Arnold Crayshaw made a speech congratulating the twins on their thirty-fifth birthday, an auspicious occasion he called it, skilfully avoiding mention of the more cogent reason for the celebration. He had dandled them on his knee, he said, playing his Dickensian role for all it was worth.

'He damn well never did,' said Blanche Courtenay loudly. 'What's the fool talkin' about? He was only Gillorn's errand boy in those days.'

Kemp smiled behind his hand; it was as good a description of an articled clerk as he'd heard.

But Blanche's words had been lost anyway for Venetia pulled Mr Crayshaw back into his seat and announced that the fireworks would start in five minutes. Chairs scraped back, and people ran to retrieve the outdoor clothes they had dropped in the hall, hung on the stairs, or pushed under their seats.

'Haven't you finished that syllabub yet?' Lettice whispered to Kemp. 'You and I have a date . . .'

It was Vivian's turn to make an announcement. The display of fireworks would take place in the courtyard at the back, and over the lake, so for this night only he had opened up the Elizabethan wing for those who did not want to brave the cold outside and could watch the fun from the windows.

The twins, together now like two tall black linked shadows, led the company down long ill-lit corridors to the rear of the premises, and out into the courtyard. The piercing cold almost hurled them back. Kemp had overheard Blanche telling her ladies that, fireworks or no fireworks, there would be coffee and hot drinks served in her upper-floor sitting-room, and he didn't blame others also for accepting that invitation.

The younger element, made more spirited by good food and wine, crowded into the courtyard already lit by smoky flares to watch the fireworks display, or wandered into the grounds to see the rockets burst across the lake. A few ventured into the Elizabethan wing itself which was colder inside than out, and gave little welcome.

Kemp was curious to see what Silas Courtenay had achieved. The heavy wooden doors had been thrown open giving access to a narrow stone-flagged passageway with rooms on either side whose tall latticed windows overlooked the courtyard and the water. The Tudor doorways were small, and the rooms themselves were bare of furnishings save for an occasional high-backed settle or an old chest against the walls, a few gnarled chairs, and some rush matting on the wooden floorboards. The air was dusty and struck chill from the stone mullions at the windows where there was more light from the clear sky and the firework display than there was inside. The dim electric bulbs strung across the low ceilings had little effect against dark panelling and heavy tapestries.

He was just thinking the place looked like an embryo museum short of funds when Lettice pulled him back into the passage. He followed her along its length to another door at the end, down a flight of stone steps into a series of caverns which must have been the kitchen department in Tudor times. He recalled from the plans he had seen that these had been rescued from ruin by Silas and partially restored, the stonework of the alcoves and fireplaces renewed. Since then nothing more had been done. From here no sound of the revels could be heard, and only dust moved in the draught from the opened door. Lettice closed it softly, and flitted away into a dark recess. He heard her lift a latch.

'It was never locked,' she said, 'I suppose the key was lost when the workmen were here, but at least there should be a light for the kitchen.' She switched it on, and swung open the low door which led to another short twisted flight of stairs just wide enough to take one person at a time.

Kemp followed the rustle of her skirts, and emerged into a small square chamber no bigger than the boxy bedroom at his own flat. There was no light here, but from a grating high on the wall the electric bulb in the kitchen shone through.

'Cosy, isn't it?' said Lettice. 'See, there are no windows, only those slits over there.' They were mere apertures in the stone, enough perhaps to get a hand through, no more. Kemp went across and put his fingers against one, and felt the cold air. 'This is an outside wall, then?'

'Just below ground level, but there's a ditch. We used to pop things through and then run outside to find them.'

Kemp glanced round, and shivered. 'Must have been bloody cold!'

'Oh, but there's a fireplace. Look . . .' She showed him the arch and the bricked-up grate. 'I suppose they brought him his food from the kitchen, and they could always keep an eye on him through that little barred window.'

'There would be rugs on the floor then,' Kemp mused, 'and some kind of hangings on the walls. There's space for a bed, a table and a chair. He had a fire, and probably lamps. There are the remains of sconces on the walls. Perhaps it wasn't so bad. Many an aristocrat sent to the Tower faced worse, and the Frenchman would know his life was in no danger. It was only a case of waiting till his relatives came up with the money.'

'Well, we mustn't wait,' said Lettice, gathering up her skirts and making for the stair.

Kemp took another look at the confined space, up at the vaulted ceiling which was high enough to level it with the roof of the kitchen above, and again at the narrow slits in the stone wall. A firework flared and something white glimmered for a second. He went over and put his hand through the aperture, and

pulled out a piece of wadded paper which had
wedged itself in a crack in a corner of the outside sill.

'Stone walls do not a prison make,
Nor iron bars a cage...'

He quoted as he went up the narrow stair. 'I've
found one of your infant letters, Lettice, that you
said you used to post.'

But Lettice wasn't listening to him. She was
standing in the kitchen, red-faced, like any schoolgirl caught in a mischievous prank.

'Lettice Warrender, what the hell are you doing in
here?'

The furious voice of Venetia Courtenay affected
Lettice as it had always done, reducing her and
causing her to stammer. 'I was only... only showing
Mr Kemp this part of the house... You know, where
we used to play hide-and-seek at Christmas, Venetia.'

Venetia's colour was high, her eyes were angry and
glinted green. But when she turned and saw Kemp
coming through the little low doorway, stooping to
avoid hitting his head on the lintel, her expression
changed, and she smiled.

'I was looking for you, Lennox,' she said sweetly,
'and here you are snooping into the secrets of our
house... How very appropriate! Or were you just
after a quick kiss and cuddle with the Lady Lettice
here? Off you go, my child. I'll look after Lennox.'

Lettice scuttled away as if she were indeed a milk-maid caught kissing the hired help. It was quite astonishing the power Venetia Courtenay had, and had probably always had since she was a girl, the arrogance which she shared with her brother, and the ability to lower one's own self-esteem; Kemp tried to feel only amused but his resentment showed. Venetia was quick to see it.

'I really have been looking for you,' she said softly. 'With all the rabble out there, I missed you. Do come with me now.'

It occurred to him that this was obviously his night for being led by women as she took his arm and drew him out of the kitchen and back along the passage-way. When they reached the courtyard a tremendous roar went up as the final set-piece of Catherine wheels and Roman fountains blazed across the metal frame erected in the grounds so that the sparkling colours lit up the lake. At the same time the last rockets burst in the sky in a shower of silver and gold. As they stood and watched, Venetia kept Kemp so close by her side that he could feel the warmth of her velvet cloak as if he was wrapped in it. She seemed in no hurry to return to the house, and ten minutes must have passed before she suggested they walk the long way round. Afterwards he could not remember what they had talked about but he did remember her laughter, the way her eyes shone silvery-green in the cold starlight, and how she never let go of his hand. If this was calculated seduction, he thought, he could not fault it. So far...

'People will be leaving now that the show is over,' she whispered, 'but don't you go, Lennox. Not yet.'

The frosted gravel in the driveway crunched beneath their feet as they came to the front of the Manor. Someone came running out of the door. Kemp recognized Dr Ambrose who had sat near him at the banquet.

'There's been an accident.' He threw the words over his shoulder. 'I must get my bag from my car.'

Kemp felt Venetia's grip tighten on his arm.

'What? In our house?'

Had he been thinking coherently and not running swiftly up the steps, Kemp might well have answered as Banquo had done: 'Too cruel, anywhere...'

There was confusion in the Great Hall at the foot of the staircase. The first thing Kemp saw was the white, anguished face of Amy Francis, the next the still figure of Lydia Beresford lying on the floor. Someone had put a cushion under her head but even with the long dress covering her legs it was obvious she lay at an awkward angle.

'The ambulance is on its way.' Lewis Proby came out of the little telephone room.

'Thank God!' came another voice. 'I saw her fall. She seemed to trip on the top step.'

Blanche Courtenay was crying.

Kemp went over to Amy. 'When did it happen?'

'Not five minutes ago. We were coming down-stairs from the sitting-room, Blanche and Prue and I were ahead. We heard Lydia talking to someone up there on the landing. Then she began to come down and... she fell...'

'Make way, ladies. Please!' Dr Ambrose stooped over Mrs Beresford and opened his bag. 'Can't we have a bit more light?'

The Hall had been cleared, the tables put away, half the lights were out. Someone found the switches. Everyone was hushed, waiting.

Dr Ambrose straightened up. 'I think she's going to be all right,' he said. 'She's concussed, of course, and she could have a broken pelvis. Those damned long skirts... You'd think a lady of her age would have more sense. Maybe a spot too much to drink...' The doctor was flustered, irritated, or he would not have spoken so. Fortunately most people had drifted away by now and there were few to hear what he muttered.

Kemp did, though, and disagreed. Lydia Beresford had taken no alcohol. 'It doesn't agree with me,' she had said. And Kemp had watched how she handled her wide dress: 'Church amateur dramatics,' she'd told him. 'We get a lot of practice.'

However, this was no time to argue the point. Kemp glanced up the staircase. It was dark at the top.

'Were there no lights up there?' he asked Amy.

'We thought we were the last to come down. Blanche put them off in her sitting-room when we left. Habit, I suppose. She said Silas had a thing about lights. And there was very little light on the stairs... Oh, my poor Lydia. It was all my fault, getting her to take part...' Amy was nearly in tears.

'Hush, Amy. It wasn't your fault. It was an accident. And you heard what Dr Ambrose said, Lydia's going to be all right. I can hear the ambulance coming now.'

Everything was competently done. The doctor fussed around his patient as the men lifted her carefully on to the stretcher and moved to the door. The flashing blue light on the ambulance roof was by now the only illumination, its purring engine the only sound where earlier all had been brilliant light and the air full of noise. When it finally left silence closed in on Courtenay Manor. The Masquerade was over.

TWELVE

KEMP WAS IN no mood to answer the telephone at eight o'clock the next morning. He hadn't got to bed till after two, and anyway it was Saturday.

'Kemp? Where were you last night?' Detective-Inspector Upshire sounded aggrieved.

'Out.'

'I know that. I've been trying to get hold of you. You keep damned late hours.'

'And this one's too early.'

'Well, that's your fault for living it up in the small hours. I want you round here at the station—pronto.'

Kemp raised himself on an elbow and tried to be reasonable.

'I'm still asleep and don't intend to wake up. Anyway, I tried to get an appointment with you yesterday.'

'I was in Court all day.'

'So they told me. They didn't seem to think my business was urgent.'

'It is now,' the Inspector growled. 'Get here.'

He banged the phone down before Kemp could ask what was all the urgency. The last time they'd spoken it was Kemp who had said they should talk further about Mrs Sorrento but Upshire, while conceding the circumstances were odd, had seen no reason for an immediate meeting. Yet here he was with his peremptory summons just when Kemp's head was particularly fragile and filled with cotton wool.

On the way back to his flat in the early hours of the morning they had called in at the hospital. Amy Francis was already there.

'I left Blanche at my house with Prue. She wouldn't stay at the Manor after what happened but she insisted that I come here to find out about Lydia.'

The night sister was sympathetic to their inquiries but guarded with her information.

'Your friend Mrs Beresford is comfortable. She was examined here in casualty and admitted with a broken pelvis as Dr Ambrose suspected. Yes, there is some concussion but her general condition is stable. I'm afraid that's all I can tell you.'

With that they had to be content.

Once inside his home Kemp had made himself coffee to warm his chilled bones, and sat for a long time going through the events of the night while they were still fresh in his mind. So many things had happened, so much had been said or left unsaid, so many fleeting impressions, they floated in and out of his consciousness like fish in a submerged forest, and would vanish unless put to the test of instant recollection. He had the sense of having been present at an illusion, a stage-show acted out behind flimsy curtains... He tried to concentrate on the realities, taking them backwards, step by step.

The last scene had been in the green and gold drawing-room upon which the remaining members of the party—family and those closely involved with it—had converged. Blanche Courtenay had sat stiffly in a chair, sipping tea, with the twins ranged on either side. Both Vivian and Venetia were at their haughtiest, sombre in their black, but unlike those present still in fancy dress, neither gave the impression of being other than what they were, perfectly at home and in their rightful place.

Arnold Crayshaw looked simply ridiculous, a crumpled Micawber, while the ladies' finery was sadly in disarray, the colour had flown from their faces, and they could only stand about like foolish waiting-women. 'Yestreen the Queen had four Maries...' The old song came back to Kemp as he saw them on entering the room.

But he was pounced upon almost immediately by Lewis Proby who, for the first time, addressed him directly.

'Ah, Mr Kemp. Did you see what happened?'

Kemp shook his head. 'No, I was outside.'

'With my wife?'

At any other time the question might have seemed either farcical or threatening, but Proby spoke as if in simple inquiry.

'As a matter of fact, yes. Did you see Mrs Beresford fall?'

'Lionel Warrender and I were in the study upstairs discussing business. We heard the commotion down here. I think she cried out. When we came out on to the landing it was dark up there. Some fool must have put the lights out . . . I didn't know her, of course. Some acquaintance of Mrs Courtenay's I believe.'

'She was my friend,' Blanche Courtenay said sharply. 'I shall go to the hospital and see her . . .'

'Later, Mother, later.' Venetia put her hand on her Mother's shoulder. 'Tonight you must stay here with us.'

'No!' Blanche's eyes sought Amy's. Amy saw the look and came over. 'Prue and I will look after your mother, Venetia. She can stay the night with me instead of at her cottage. I agree she should not be alone.' Amy had regained her self-control and spoke decisively. Blanche had risen and allowed Amy to take her arm. Others had followed as if thankful at last to have an excuse for leaving. The twins had watched in order of their going with the same expression of lordly indifference they had assumed since the accident happened, as if it had been no concern of theirs, indeed might have been reprehensible behaviour in that it had cast a blight on their festivities.

Common courtesy—an odd phrase in the circumstances—had demanded that Kemp pay his dues on departure, so he had walked across to his host and hostess and murmured polite nothings. They had been standing very close to one another as if for mutual support, and when Venetia had held out her hand to him it was cold. So were her eyes, a cold stony grey with no light in them. Vivian, despite his lofty bearing, had seemed racked by inner unease, his fingers twisting nervously below the falls of lace at the wrists, and for once he had had nothing to say.

Now, as Kemp prepared for the day ahead, that picture of them came back into his mind. What had they done, these two, when the guests had gone? Of course Lewis Proby was there, and some of their London friends would have stayed over... Kemp realized how little he really knew of the twins' lives, apart from their brief excursions into his—and even in these their attitude had been enigmatic...

They're another species, he said to himself, these Courtenay twins, they inhabit a wilder shore than mine, and they move to a tune of their own... Yet why had they involved him in their dance? Why was he feeling now in the cold light of day that he had been manipulated? He'd had that fleeting fancy last night when he'd been led, first by Lettice Warrender and then by Venetia, down those long dark corridors. And it had happened before: he had been led to meet Venetia, and she in turn had led him over the lawns to that seat where they had talked... Was he a bit player in some tortuous game?

It was a startling thought and one that stopped him in his tracks.

Then he told himself briskly that he was being too imaginative, carried away as Elvira might have said by the razzle-dazzle of high society. Better get back to reality and keep a clear head to hear what John Upshire had to say on the sordid tale of the Sorrentos. He reached for casual clothing as it was his weekend off and he'd no intention of even appearing to be on official business at the police station. Not the heavy jacket he'd worn the night before and been glad of in those chilly early hours, but a lighter one. He put a hand in the pocket to transfer his wallet and brought out with it the piece of wadded paper he'd found in the crack in the stone. He unfolded the creases and spread it out. It looked as if it had been torn from a pad, and all that was written on it, in pencil, was: *11.30, Thursday*.

This wasn't any of Lettice's childish notes left there from some Christmas past, the scrap of paper was recent, folded as if to tuck into a pocket-book as a reminder of an appointment. But why there, in that abandoned room?

Kemp put it carefully in his own wallet, and walked round to the Newtown Police Station.

'Well,' he said to John Upshire when they were both seated in the Inspector's room, 'what fresh development in the Sorrento saga makes you wake me at eight in the morning?'

'Something damn serious. You remember I checked the airlines and found Mrs Sorrento was never booked on any flight after the inquest?'

'Yes, you told me. That's why I wanted to talk.'

'You can talk right now,' growled Upshire. 'The airline acted very responsibly, I'll say that for them. I'd only asked about flights in September and they didn't find her on any of them, but the next day they checked again *before* the dates I'd given them, and do you know what?'

'I can't even guess.'

The Inspector paused and took a deep breath.

'Not just Mrs Julie Sorrento, but her husband and the two children all flew to Sicily on August 24th.'

'But that's impossible! She came to see me on the 26th... I know now they weren't her children she had with her, but...' He stopped, taking in the whole of what Upshire had said. 'You mean Luciano Sorrento was also on that plane?'

'That's what the airline said. They keep good records. The whole family left Heathrow on that date in August.'

'So either it was another woman on that flight,' said Kemp slowly, picking his words, 'or it wasn't Julie Sorrento who came into my office.'

'I don't give a damn who came into your office. What worries me is him—Luciano.'

Both men stared at each other, and Upshire nodded, grim-faced.

'My God!' exclaimed Kemp. 'If it really was Luciano Sorrento who travelled with his family out of England on that date, whose body was it in the clay-pit?'

'Got it in one.' Upshire heaved a deep sigh. 'Identified by his wife, or a woman who was or was not his wife, and if she was his wife, she was in Sicily at the time, and if she wasn't his wife, then who the hell was she?' It was no wonder his tone had turned sour. 'There wasn't any need for forensics, fingerprints, dentistry, all the paraphernalia we'd have gone through with an unknown corpse. Oh, no, it all went so smoothly. Husband missing, even reported missing by wife to his employers, to the social services, and to a bright, clever solicitor like yourself. And then she positively identifies the body...'

'There's no chance they could have come back, minus the children?' Kemp was groping in the dark as much as the Inspector.

Upshire shook his head. 'There's no record they did. Anyway, why should they? Whatever they'd been up to, the Sorrentos—and I'll wager it was something pretty nasty—it was finished. And we're left with an unidentified body that was duly buried with all the rites of the Roman Catholic Church...'

Kemp was trying to see his way through to the consequences.

'This means exhumation?'

Upshire closed his eyes at the very thought.

'Might come to that—with all it entails... But there's that inquest verdict to contend with—death by misadventure. That'll not be easily overturned. Murder was never even suspected.'

'You're checking Sicily, of course?'

'Don't teach your granny to suck eggs, Lennox. Of course we're checking Sicily, but that'll take weeks if I know the Italian police. And what have we got in actual evidence against the Sorrentos? Deception of some kind, probably, but not much else—hardly an extraditable offence.'

Kemp's thoughts were racing but not as yet towards any recognizable finishing line.

'The answer to all the questions we're asking now lies with the real identity of that man who was found in the claypit,' he said carefully. 'Someone went to great trouble to make us believe it was Luciano Sorrento. If Sorrento's still alive and well in Sicily, then we have to start looking at the whole set-up from a different angle.'

'And that's just where you come in.' John Upshire sat up straighter, and looked keener. 'What's all this stuff you've been raking up about the woman who may or not be Julie Sorrento, and the kids you now say weren't hers?'

So Kemp told him, right from the beginning.

When he'd finished he knew the narrative had been a poor thing of shreds and patches, lacking any decent wrapping of sense, and that it had raised more queries than it answered. He felt himself hampered by gnawing resentment, an angry frustration which was not helped by the Inspector's sardonic comments.

'She fooled you too, this woman in the Rastafarian ringlets. At least she'd combed these out by

the time I took her to the inquest . . .' John Upshire
was pleased that he wasn't the only one to have been
duped. He had been known to pass the opinion that
there were times when Lennox Kemp was too clever
for his own good.

WPC Prentiss had been called in, and appealed to.
She was bewildered, but stubborn. 'There were others at that inquest, sir, who knew her as Mrs Sorrento. I heard one of Everetts' men call her that.'

'But they hardly knew her before,' said Kemp.
'She didn't mix much with the other workers or their
wives, and they would expect her to be Mrs Sorrento. Besides, an appearance in Court is apt to make
people look quite different from their normal. What
colour were her eyes, Miss Prentiss?'

The policewoman frowned. 'Darkish, I think, but
not easy to make out under that fringe.' She turned
to the Inspector. 'Wasn't she Mrs Sorrento, sir?'

He shrugged. 'Blessed if I know. If it wasn't, it was
someone who knew her.'

'And was made-up to look like her?' said Miss
Prentiss. 'She'd be easy to copy. You talking about
an actress?'

It was a perceptive comment. 'Do you think it
possible, Miss Prentiss?' Kemp was interested to
know.

'Well . . . she was a type. The slight Cockney accent would be easy . . . everybody's seen *My Fair
Lady* . . . Then that hair, all over the place, you can
get wigs like that. And, as for colour of eyes, there's

always contact lenses if you're really serious about it. The sort of clothes? Well, she could've been wearing the real Mrs Sorrento's . . .'

'Why did you say *My Fair Lady*?' asked Kemp.

'I don't really know. It just came into my head. I mean, that was about a low-class girl turned into a lady. You could do it the other way round, couldn't you?' WPC Prentiss found Kemp staring at her. 'Have I said something wrong?'

'No. You may have said something right. Thank you very much.'

When she had gone, Upshire looked shrewdly at Kemp. 'You've had an idea?'

Kemp shook his head as if by doing so the idea might rattle into place so that he could pursue it at another time.

'Can we go over those dates again?' he said. 'I want to compare them with my own notes when I go back to my office.'

The Inspector obliged.

According to the Italian airline, the Sorrento family had flown to Sicily on Monday, August 24. On Wednesday, August 26, Julie Sorrento—for want of a better name for her—had called at Kemp's office with two children she had 'borrowed' for the day. She reported her husband, Luciano, as missing from the previous Friday, August 19, which tallied with the last time he was seen by his fellow-workers at Everetts. On September 12 a body was found in the claypit at Burrow Hill. Pathological evidence at the inquest said that death must have occurred at some time during the preceding two weeks.

'Two weeks?' Kemp queried sharply.

The Inspector looked at his file. 'That's what the report said. But in his evidence at the inquest Dr More allowed it could have happened earlier. There had been considerable rainfall at the end of August, and the body was in a state of some decomposition. He would stretch a point to make it possibly three weeks...'

'Bringing it rather neatly back to the date of Luciano's original disappearance over the weekend of the 20th, and by Mrs Sorrento's statement that her husband stayed out nights anyway up there at the old allotment site.'

'And the Sorrento birds flew the coop four days later,' said Upshire triumphantly, 'having murdered their man—whoever he was—and making sure the body wouldn't be found until they were out of the country. They might just have got away with it,' he added, rubbing his chin, 'if I hadn't checked the airlines...'

'Which you only did because I was poking my nose in,' Kemp observed, mildly, 'but that simple scenario doesn't answer the question why there was all this rigmarole of reporting a missing husband. If the Sorrentos had just killed someone by chucking him over the edge of that pit, why call attention to it? Why not simply scarper?'

The Inspector was a little slower in the uptake, but he got there in the end.

'Someone else wanted the body found?'

'Oh, the body would have been found anyway. You know that. Burrow Hill isn't a particularly isolated spot, and the body wasn't even buried, was it? And look at all the hints we were given. Luciano's love for his allotment, his drinking and mooning about up there... Yes, the body was meant to be found all right, and identified as his. That was the whole point of the exercise. Are you following me?'

'Only just. Why, if Luciano was still alive, did the Sorrentos plan to have the corpse identified as his? And a bloody elaborate plan too, for an Italian tomato-worker and an ill-educated female...'

Kemp raised a hand in protest.

'Plots have been hatched before by just such ill-assorted couples. But that's not the point. The Julie Sorrento both you and I met might simply have been playing dumb, though I have to agree with you that, by the sparse accounts given by other witnesses who knew the real one, I think she was in fact just that. How about this mother of hers in Camden Town?'

The Inspector glared. 'What do you take us for? Of course we've investigated that side. Checked the marriage records. Julie Sorrento—the real one—married Luciano Sorrento five years ago in—would you believe it? Camden Town. Her maiden name was Morgan. What a blessing the Department of Employment is!' He cocked an eye at Kemp, 'After you stirred things up, you see, I set some inquiries going. Julie Sorrento checks the whole way through: she'd a series of jobs after leaving school, ending up six years ago when she came to Newtown as a packer in the brush factory. She married her Italian a year later, putting an end to her not very illustrious commercial career.'

'And Mother Morgan to whom she used to repair with the children when marital bliss wore off?'

The Inspector consulted his file. 'Full marks to the Met boys, they got on to that one right away when I phoned them last night, just a civil inquiry... But it wasn't difficult finding her, same address as on the marriage certificate, Peabody Buildings number 55, and Grandma Morgan still lives there.'

'So?'

It was Upshire's turn to protest. 'Hey, give us time! Let's see ... A Sergeant Hunt went to see Mrs Morgan last night. She confirmed yes, she had a daughter Julie, married to an Italian called Sorrento. She wasn't too keen on him on account of him being of the Catholic persuasion, but, yes, Julie brought Maria and Luke to see her often. According to Hunt, memory isn't her strong point, and she isn't very bright, either. Sometime in August was the last time she'd seen Julie, couldn't remember the date. What she did remember was Julie telling her they were all going off to Sicily, might be for a holiday, might be for good...'

'When?'

'She couldn't remember.'

'What about round the time of the inquest—did her daughter go to her then with the children?'

'I told you, Mrs Morgan said she hadn't seen her daughter since that time in August. One interesting thing, though: she didn't know Luciano was either missing, or dead. She's got bad eyesight, and doesn't read the newspapers or watch the telly. Sergeant Hunt was told to be careful over that. He told her nothing but he says in his report she never mentioned a funeral or anything like that but spoke of Luciano as if he was still around, though she never had a good word to say of him anyway—for the above-mentioned reason. Look, Lennox, I'd no reason to have my colleagues in the Mets harass the woman...'

'Of course not. Sorry. At least we know where the real Julie Sorrento came from, and it was true about her taking off with the children from time to time to visit her ma. I don't suppose we can learn any more from that quarter. In fact, I think everything in her life up to August tallies with what I've learned from that neighbour on the caravan site, from Luciano's fellow-workers, and from Annie Mungo. There was nothing mysterious, nothing sinister about the real Julie Sorrento...'

'H'mm. I see from Sergeant Hunt's report he even saw the postcard Mrs Morgan had from her daughter. Blue skies and sunshine. "Having a good time,

Love, Julie''... He checked the postmark, dated last week.'

'I know. I know. Just like the one Mrs Mungo had.' Kemp got up to go. 'I think we shall find all the Sorrento family are in Sicily enjoying the blue skies and sunshine. The birds have gone South for the winter—or for good.'

'That doesn't solve my problem.' The Inspector rose heavily to his feet. 'I've still got an unidentified corpse on my hands.'

Kemp turned at the door.

'Tell me, what's a murderer's biggest headache?'

John Upshire considered it. 'Getting rid of the body.'

'That's it,' said Kemp. 'Unless you can make it someone else's body.'

THIRTEEN

KEMP MAY have given a jaunty impression to Inspector Upshire but when he emerged into the unconcerned streets of Newtown at eleven o'clock on a Saturday morning, he was not light-hearted. He seethed with emotions, the strongest being anger, which bid fair to swamp all others.

Of course he should have spoken out, given some voice to his suspicions. The police, under Upshire's direction, would have their duties: the first, to investigate all missing persons in the vicinity, for a nameless corpse must answer to some vacancy in living. Inquiries would go all the way down through disappearances of malcontent husbands, absconding clerks, amnesiacs and disaffected adolescents to the sub-strata of itinerant labourers and tramps who might otherwise not be missed for months...

But, he argued, it wasn't as if he really knew anything. All he had was this bit of paper. It was enough, however, to make him go straight to the Public Library before it closed at twelve o'clock.

It was quiet, the populace of Newtown having better things to do with its leisure than plan the weekend's reading. Mrs Beresford's table by the window was of course vacant, and there was only one lethargic young woman at the main desk.

'Mrs Beresford? Oh, she never comes in of a Saturday. Anyway, I hear she's been involved in an accident and is in hospital... Can I help you?' This last offer made without much enthusiasm.

'Not really.' Kemp was at a loss. 'I just wanted to know... Someone had an appointment with her. To go over some Parish registers.' As he spoke Kemp had strolled over to Lydia's table. He glanced down at the almost bare surface. Neatly arranged in a glass tray were pencils, and beside it a blank pad. 'What a lot of pencils she has!' he exclaimed.

'They have to have pencils,' said the girl, 'they're not allowed pens or ballpoints when looking at the old registers. They used to get marked something terrible, the records I mean, so the archivist has a rule now—only pencils allowed.'

'That makes sense,' said Kemp, marking time while he abstracted the piece of paper from his wallet. 'Funny how people come from all over the globe just to find out who their ancestors were. Might be better in some cases to let well alone.'

'That's what I say,' the girl said. She had a pile of books on the desk in front of her and was jabbing a red-painted nail into her computer. 'I mean, what's the good of finding your great-great-grandfather was hanged for sheepstealing? Me, I'd rather not know, thank you very much.'

She was intent on her task, and took no notice of what Kemp was doing. He didn't look as if he was out to steal books, just standing idly looking down at Mrs Beresford's desk. He had laid his scrap of paper on top of the memo pad; it fitted exactly.

'Not that I don't admire her work,' the girl was going on 'I mean, she does it voluntary, like, she's not paid to do it.' She made this sound either worthy of civic recognition or the height of folly.

Kemp strolled back to her. 'I hope Mrs Beresford soon recovers from her accident. I won't trouble you any further.'

Standing on the steps outside the library in the pale sunshine, he was suddenly imbued with a new and awful lucidity of vision. The skyline of Newtown, as banal as any in Britain, struck his eyesight with such startling intensity that it might have been a painted backdrop. As he walked the familiar streets it came to him that lately he had been caught up in someone else's malevolent dream, whereas this was the real world, these crowds popping in and out of the eye-catching shopfronts with bulging bags and baby buggies were his people and his job was to deal with the present; not any pseudo-romantic past nor grandiloquent exploitable future, but the here-and-now, no matter how distasteful . . .

At least these sober thoughts had cooled his anger by the time he had opened up the empty office, poured himself coffee and looked out the Sorrento file. He put the scrap from the library memo pad

bearing the pencilled reminder *Thursday 11.30* into
the file because there wasn't anywhere else to put it.

He hadn't been asked to open a file on any missing American. Indeed, he might well not be missing
at all. His interest in 'family' might have evapo-
rated, he could have moved on. He might be anywhere in England, anywhere in Europe by now, they
traversed the globe, these wandering Americans,
even those on walking holidays and not affluent...
They would stay in bed-and-breakfast accommodation or hostels, they might hitch-hike their way across
the country...

But this one had gone to Courtenay Manor, he'd
done more than simply look over the castle wall, he'd
left his mark within. Some of the words of 'Little Sir
Hugh' rattled about in Kemp's mind:

He kicked the ball so very high
He kicked the ball so low...
He kicked it over the castle wall
Where no one dared to go...

And this American had an Italian name, he was
dark and olive-skinned. A description which also
fitted Luciano Sorrento, who might yet turn out to
be alive and well in the sunshine of Sicily despite
having been duly laid to rest in Newtown Cemetery
after a properly conducted inquest. That, however,
was the Inspector's problem; the wheels might grind
slow, but grind they would in the end. Of course

John Upshire wouldn't have the necessary clout to make finding the Sorrentos top priority for the Sicilian police—they weren't part of an international spy ring and there'd been no hint of narcotics—so he might well have to wait weeks before they could be questioned . . .

Kemp stared at the other notes on the file. That visit of the brother, Alfredo. He'd told the Inspector about that . . . but not the other item he'd learned from Annie Mungo, for it hadn't seemed important at the time. That, during Alfredo's holiday, there had been a supper party in Newtown, the Sorrentos and the Courtenay twins . . .

It seemed too tenuous a link to take seriously, but it was the only one . . . No, it wasn't . . . There was himself. At the thought which now stared him in the face, he felt the anger he had tried to crush rise again so that he got up and kicked his chair over. If he accepted the premise—sickening in its implications—that he had been used from the beginning, manipulated and led by the nose, then other things fell into place. Somehow or other, he had been made part of, even the pivot of, a plot, for which he had been lined up and set on his course like a blind horse . . . He got up, and put the chair straight.

This conclusion, reached by instinct rather than reason, not only made him angry, it also left him profoundly unhappy. There was the hurt to his *amour propre* as well as general disgruntlement at his own lack of perception from the very beginning. But anger and resentment were no help now. He must resort to rational thinking, take reasonable steps, not fly off the handle and charge at a bewilderment of windmills...

He decided to play it softly, softly. He would go and see Lionel Warrender to find out what was going on between him and Lewis Proby. Lettice answered the phone at Castleton House; yes, her father was on the golf-course but he would be home when the light faded.

Kemp had never found the conversation of stock-brokers, even those with flair for the business, particularly rewarding at weekends and Lionel, who lacked that edge, was a dull dog at the best of times but he'd had a good round that afternoon so was in an expansive mood.

He was not aware that he was being gently quizzed over the toasted tea-cakes in front of the fire, though Lettice, who knew Kemp better, could have told him so.

'They underestimate Lewis, the Courtenays,' Lionel said, 'just because he took a plunge a few years back. Could happen to anyone...'

Kemp was quick to sympathize; he knew it had once happened to Lionel. 'But Lewis Proby held on?' he said.

'He's just the man for doing that,' said Lionel, with enthusiasm. 'He kept his head, and waited. He knew the opportunity would come, and now it has.'

'He has a project in view?'

Lionel laid a finger along a nose still glowing from the cold wind and now reddened by the fire. 'Keeping it hush-hush for the moment, of course, but it's a winner. Lewis has got the planners on his side, and the local landowners... And, more important, he has access to City money... They'll all go for it round here. Young Courtenay, now, he's been a fool, he's antagonized everybody up at County Hall, and I dare say your lot as well, eh, Lettice?'

'I know nothing at all about it, Dad,' said Lettice, handing cake, but she winked at Kemp, who took no notice.

'Mr Proby is only the secretary of V. & V. Enterprises,' remarked Kemp. 'I don't see him having much influence there...'

Lionel waved that aside as being of little importance. 'Lewis is forming his own company. Local shareholders, you know. Those with a proper interest in the land. It'll be a gentleman's club. Just what Newtown needs...'

'You mean a golf-course?' Kemp was beginning to see why Lionel Warrender was so engaged; at the moment he had to travel to the next county for a decent game.

Lionel nodded. 'For the benefit of Newtown, naturally.'

'I still don't quite see...' Kemp hesitated. 'I mean, I think it's a great idea...but surely it's up to the Courtenays?'

At that point Lionel became more reticent, and it was only after much diplomatic probing and questioning on Kemp's part that he was able to get a clear picture of the scheme being hatched by Lewis Proby. The way Lionel looked at it, the Courtenays would come round in the end when they found their own harebrained plans balked at every turn by local feeling and the stringencies of the planning laws.

Kemp took a different view. As he drove away from Castletown House, he knew he had been right to come. It was not that he cared very deeply about the future of the Manor lands—he didn't play golf and had never felt the need for a gentleman's club even had he been eligible—but he had had confirmed what he already suspected, that Lewis Proby was a very dark horse indeed, and one about to emerge from the stables under new colours. Moreover, from what Lionel Warrender did not say, or rather what he stumbled on in the saying—for he was not a man who dissembled easily—it was obvious that neither of the Courtenay twins knew anything of this new development.

According to Lionel, 'they were about to get their come-uppance, these two...' When Kemp had raised inquiring eyebrows at the phrase, Lionel had muttered that the words had been Lewis Proby's. He thought they referred to them coming a cropper over planning consents. To Kemp the words had a darker meaning. Lewis Proby was hinting at their downfall...and he was getting out from under. He was not only getting out, he was taking something with him and that to a man like Proby could only mean one thing: Money...

Proby, it seemed, had waited long enough. But, even if Venetia was still his wife, there was nothing in it for him, as there had been nothing in the long years of waiting for her expectations to be realized... From what Kemp knew of her, she was hardly likely to give hand-outs even now to a husband she so obviously despised. No, this had to be something else, something that, for once, had given Proby the upper hand. He had a lever on the twins, and now only waited the opportunity to pull it.

Such cogitations, although without any proper conclusion, lasted Kemp the drive back to his flat where he found, behind the door, a note from Amy Francis. She had tried unsuccessfully to reach him by telephone, and he had not been in when she called. If he returned by the evening would he come to supper with her and Blanche?

Kemp phoned Amy immediately. It was kind of them to invite him and he would be with them in an hour. As he changed, he thought about Blanche Courtenay. She did not seem to have ever had an excess of motherly instinct, yet her flight from the Manor once the son and daughter had taken control showed remarkable determination to distance herself from them.

There was no doubt she was more at ease in Amy's company than with her own family, and looking at her now across the supper table Kemp was struck by the fact that she even seemed younger, as though she had thrown off a burden of years.

They were all relieved by the news from the hospital; Lydia Beresford was out of danger, and was being prepared for an operation on Monday to pin the broken pelvis.

'She still doesn't remember what actually happened on the staircase,' said Amy. 'The doctor said that's quite normal with concussion, but she's healthy and the break will heal.'

'Those lights on the landing...' Blanche was frowning as she spoke. 'Far too high up, and always so dim, but Silas had always been so stingy about electricity. If only Lydia hadn't been the last to come down...'

'She wasn't the last,' explained Kemp. 'Mr Proby and Lionel Warrender were still in the study upstairs. They came out when they heard all the commotion, and Lionel told me there were other people on the landing when they arrived. Don't worry about it, Mrs Courtenay, it was just an unfortunate accident.' He didn't really believe that, but this was neither the time nor the place to voice doubt.

He steered the conversation in other directions and inevitably it turned to horses. Blanche Courtenay was not by nature a talkative woman; she would make terse comments and leave them there. But once on to her own subject she could be quite a racy raconteur and displayed a surprisingly earthy sense of humour, learnt presumably from grooms and stable lads.

Amy had brought out a good wine but, as Kemp intended to drive home, he drank little of it, leaving the second bottle to the ladies. By the end of the meal Blanche had sufficiently relaxed to speak of her early days when she had been, as she put it, 'one of the Daubeny gurls.'

'Father had racing stables at Newmarket. Spent all our time there. Never out of the saddle... The string goin' out on the downs on a misty morning...' She gave a sigh at the memory, her words the closest she could get to lyricism.

'But Charles, your husband, he didn't ride?' asked Amy.

'His brother Silas thought horses only fit for pulling coal carts. And they cost money...' Blanche brooded on that for a moment. 'Anyway, Charles was away at the war.'

'You were engaged when you were very young, Mrs Courtenay,' Kemp remarked.

'Just turned eighteen. Never gave it a thought. All arranged, you know, between the families. Mine saw it as a good match—all those Courtenay millions!' She gave a little laugh, without any perceptible bitterness. 'Pa was down on his luck by then... But Charles and I got on well enough. He said when he came into the estate he'd give me all the geegees I wanted. It never worked out. I got the twins instead.'

There was an uncomfortable silence but Blanche
seemed unaware of it. She drank some more wine,
put down her glass and gazed into it. Then she went
on speaking but more to herself than the company.
'Charles would have kept his part of the bargain, as
I kept mine. Always the gentleman, Charles, always
did the honourable thing. Even with that poor creature in America... Damn the Courtenay Trust! How
was Charles to know the old miser'd live for ever?'

Her voice had slurred, her speech was becoming
disconnected, but Kemp had pricked up his ears.
'The Trust... yes,' he said carefully, 'Mr Archie let
me see the papers. You were not treated fairly.'

Blanche turned her large pale eyes upon him. They
were grey like her daughter's but without the lively
spark of green. Kemp couldn't make out whether she
was actually seeing him or some figure from the past.

She slowly shook her head. 'Fair? 'Course it
wasn't fair, but what'd you expect from a bunch of
mealy-mouthed lawyers? Saving your presence, Mr
Kemp.'

She was spryer than he had thought. He would
have to lead this one gently like a thoroughbred, for
that, after all, was what Blanche Courtenay was. If
he muffed it she would pull up her head, toss away
the rein and be off. He was aware of Amy's watchful stillness, and wondered if she too saw the anal-
ogy.

He made it sound casual, simply a part of general conversation, as he leaned back and played with his coffee spoon. 'Archie told me your husband had a good war. Didn't he end up in Washington with some military mission?'

'Army stuff.' Blanche dismissed it. 'None of my business.' Her wine glass was empty, and Amy quietly refilled it. 'I like to hear you talk about Charles, Blanche,' she said, smiling at her friend. 'You so rarely do.'

'What's there to say? It was such a long time ago...' But as if she could not let go the thread of her reminiscence, Blanche went on: 'Must have been the summer of 'forty-five he went... Damned cold huntin' the next winter, I remember. Easter wedding all fixed up by Mama, thankful that was the last of us off her hands... Charles came home. He'd had his fling. Told no one but me. Thought it was the decent thing to do—always did the decent thing, Charles. Little Italian gurl he'd met in a bar in New York, only knew her a few months and then she's dead...'

'Oh, Blanche!' exclaimed Amy. 'You must have been so upset...'

'No, I wasn't,' said Blanche firmly, 'I thought it quite romantic. I wasn't what you'd call in love with Charles, nor he with me, though we were good friends. Anyway, it was over, and the poor thing was dead of septicaemia. Insanitary place, New York...'

No matter how much wine she took, it appeared that Blanche could go through these phases of incoherence and muddle to suddenly emerge robustly sober. Kemp had noticed it the first time he had met her at the Manor, and here she was doing it again.

'Did any of the family ever know?' he asked her.

'Certainly not. It was a matter strictly between Charles and me. He promised me my horses, and I promised to keep quiet.' Blanche reached for her glass, and chuckled. 'Can you imagine how that little episode would've gone down with Silas and the trustees? They'd have had the staggers!'

'You said Venetia had been asking you about her father quite recently,' said Amy.

'Badgering me, more like.' At the mention of her daughter Blanche's eyes glazed, and her face crumpled. 'I did tell her. She kept going on and on about him . . . How most men have affairs before they're married, and he'd be no exception. I owed it to poor Charles's memory to tell her the truth, that it wasn't like that. Not like the way she said it... I wanted her to know that her father believed in honour, and he did the correct thing by that gurl before she died.' Blanche looked defiantly across at Amy. 'Wasn't I right to tell her?'

'Of course you were, Blanche,' Amy responded warmly.

'She only scoffed, said what a fool he'd been . . . I told her to get out of my house. I wouldn't have her talk about her father like that... Oh, why did Charles have to die so soon?' Blanche gave a sudden wailing cry. 'He was the best of the lot of them. How I hate my children!'

Amy gave Kemp an appealing look. Blanche had put her head down on the table, and the cloth was wet with her tears.

Kemp knew it was time he left. But he had to find out before he went. He put his hand very gently on Blanche's shoulder. 'Did Charles ever tell you the name of the girl?'

Her voice was muffled, but she spoke up.

'We'd no secrets from each other. Of course he told me, though it didn't matter by then. Rosina she was called, and the other name like it. Rossi, that was it. Charles was so sorry for her when she was ill...and then her family took her away from him and she died ... And my poor Charles was dead himself within the year...'

Blanche was crying again, and Amy took Kemp firmly by the arm and hustled him out.

'I'll see she gets a good rest,' she told him at the door. 'Perhaps it wasn't a good idea to let her run on like that. I'm sure she didn't really mean what she said just now about the twins.'

'I think she did,' said Kemp. 'It was a hard thing to say but it was probably true. Remember, she was very young and inexperienced, and in her own way she loved her husband. His death was a tragedy the twins could never make up for.'

'And did you get what you came for tonight, Lennox?' Amy's blue eyes were stern.

'I came because you asked me to, Amy,' Kemp replied lightly, but he knew she didn't believe him.

FOURTEEN

THERE WAS ONLY one last thing to do. Kemp had spent most of the night putting the pieces together. They fitted. Of course there were still vast areas of ignorance, and Kemp had found that these expanded as his circles of knowledge widened just as if one was blowing up a balloon, the outer skin touching more and more edges of space into which he had not penetrated. He had discovered this to be a phenomenon of all his cases but, although the concept was intriguing, he had never let it stop him going for the centre from which all else flowed. And now that centre was Courtenay Manor.

It was again a Sunday morning, but neither so soft nor so blandly sunlit as on the previous occasion. The frost that had come on the night of November 5 had hardened into a bleak coldness which took all colour from the landscape, leaving it dull and lifeless as though struck by an iron fist. There was scarcely enough moisture in the air to make the hedges white nor the roads icy, just a grey dryness of atmosphere which fixed bush and tree into sculpted stone.

That was how the Manor looked when he reached it, like a cardboard castle built for a film set. He had thought of telephoning first, then decided against it. He had been busy enough on the telephone at his flat before he left.

It was early, not yet ten o'clock, but a car swung out of the drive as he braked at the entrance. Had he missed them altogether? But it was Lewis Proby whom he glimpsed at the wheel. In the back he recognized the housekeeper, and two of the maids. Was this the break-up of the household?

He parked his car behind the same laurel bush out of which Venetia's voice had seemed to come that other morning. He crunched over the gravel and up the steps to the front door. Perhaps by now there was no one at home, yet as he pulled at the great bell which must have been there in Silas Courtenay's time and heard its sonorous peal, he felt in his bones that someone would answer.

It took a long five minutes before there were footsteps in the hall, and the heavy door creaked on its hinges as it opened.

Vivian was in a dressing-gown with gold and green dragons on it, a garment Noël Coward would have taken pride in.

'Hullo, Kemp. A bit early for a business call, eh?'

'I'd like a word with you and your sister—if it's not inconvenient.'

'Liberty Hall, old chap. Though you might have warned us you were coming...' But he stood aside and allowed Kemp to enter. He for his part was reflecting, sardonically, that this was where the higher

classes always scored. Civilities that came naturally
to them they used like weapons. Vivian might be a
puppy but he was a well-schooled puppy. Manners
makyth man...

He followed him through to the green drawing-
room, to which the harsh morning light was no
kinder than it had been to the fields outside. Venetia
rose gracefully and greeted him as if he were an expected guest; perhaps not one entirely welcome but
none the less expected. She was wearing something
vaguely resembling a riding habit although he knew
she didn't ride, a cream silk shirt and tight sand-
coloured corduroy trousers, a brilliant orange scarf
at her neck, and her blonde hair scraped back into a
pony-tail. Your lady of the manor at leisure on a
Sunday morning, ready for anything from a visiting
person to a television interviewer.

'Lennox? How lovely... Do join us for coffee.' She
glanced towards Vivian hesitating in the doorway.

'We'll have to make it ourselves,' he grumbled.
'Your precious Lewis seems to have removed the
staff.'

'It's their Sunday off, as you very well know.
Lewis said he'd drive them into town.' There was an
edge to her voice, a hint of some underlying irritation, perhaps concern at the servants' defection—or
Proby's. 'Surely you can use a percolator, brother
dear? And there's that special blend Lennox is sure
to like. He must get so tired of that awful stuff out

of his office machine. Go on, Viv, let us entertain our visitor in style.'

Vivian went, reluctantly, and Venetia gestured to Kemp that he should take a seat. He preferred to stand, however, or walk about the room while he talked. There was only one way to deal with all this spurious polite behaviour, and that was to override it.

'Talking of visitors, Mrs Proby, did you have an American here at the Manor sometime—um—late August, early September?'

Venetia's eyes were silvery clear today, so was her laugh. 'Americans? Really, how could one tell? You've seen the crowds we have here... Friends bring friends, you know. We don't ask for their passports!'

'His name was Carlos E. Rossi. Carlos Ember Rossi. And he has disappeared.'

'So what? Isn't that the usual American response? So succinct, so very expansive. Just a degree above monkey language.'

'He came here to the Manor. I know that for a fact. He left his calling card.'

'How thoughtful of him,' she said sweetly, 'An American with a sense of etiquette. Now that would have been a real catch, wouldn't it? But, sorry, Lennox, I've never heard of your Mr Rossi. He sounds like an ice-cream parlour...'

Kemp stopped pacing backwards and forwards, and confronted her.

'Venetia. I'm serious. Carlos Rossi was here, and I know why he came.'

She waved her arms languidly about her head. 'Search me. Again, how laconic their language is... And what a silly old sleuth you are, Lennox Kemp. But then that's your metier, isn't it? You live like the earthworm, a blind creature that feeds on dung-hills...' The abrupt change in her tone from light frivolity to a deadly hiss sent Kemp back on his heels, and, before he could recover she was calling gaily across the room to Vivian.

'Ah, coffee—as they say in those adverts. I hope you found the best beans, brother mine.'

She waited till Vivian had put the tray down— which he did with little ceremony—before she went on: 'Mr Kemp has been inquiring whether we know of an American called Carlos something or other. Apparently he's mislaid him.' She was setting out the cups and her voice was casual but Kemp sensed the warning in it and trained his eyes on Vivian. He would have less control than his sister.

Vivian's hand had gone to the cravat at his throat, the fine long fingers pulling at the satin as if it had suddenly tightened. He turned quickly and walked over to the window. 'Never heard of him,' he said. 'Can't stand Americans. Too loud-mouthed for my liking.'

'This one wasn't,' said Kemp calmly, as he fol-lowed him. 'He was a pleasant, well-spoken young man about the same age as yourself, Mr Courtenay.'

'Oh, come along, you two. Stop wandering around. Sit down and let's have coffee like civilized beings.' The hard edge was back in her voice.

'I don't want any bloody coffee. I'm going up-stairs to dress.'

There was no way Kemp could prevent the master of the house from striding out of his own drawing-room, but he was unhappy to see him go. Vivian, as the weaker of the two, would have been easier to tackle.

Kemp stood for a moment gazing out of the long window at the empty urns on the terrace, the un-pruned roses hanging their dead heads over the fro-zen earth; it could have been a graveyard. Behind him came the tinkling sound of cups and saucers.

'Forgive my brother's lack of manners. Won't you join me? You make me nervous marching about like that.'

He turned, walked over to the sofa opposite her and sat down, the small marble-topped table be-tween them. 'You have reason to be nervous,' he said pleasantly, as he accepted the cup she held out to him.

'Milk? Sugar?'

'No, thanks. I'll take it black.'

'To match your mood? You're no longer being amusing, Lennox.' She tried the pretty pout, but it was only a twist of the lips. Her eyes had darkened. Lacking their natural mobility, her fine patrician features showed the strain of a steely self-control.

Kemp sipped his coffee. It was bitter, as he knew it would be. Did he really have to go through with this charade? Inspector Upshire had told him he was mad...

'The way I see it, Venetia,' he said, leaning back comfortably on the cushions, 'is that Carlos Rossi came here one day last August. His middle name was Ember and he was looking for his ancestors who were English. He was directed to the village of Ember. Americans on holiday talk to everybody—even the local gentry. I think he wandered up to the Manor...'

Venetia burst out laughing, no longer a silvery sound but metallic.

'What a very romantic tale! But what on earth has it to do with us? People come and go here as they like—even Americans. We don't keep a register of guests. Why, he might even have been at one of our house-parties, perhaps the very one to which you came, Lennox, when I met you first and thought it might be the beginning of something wonderful...' She was mocking now. 'You might even have seen him that night, your wandering minstrel...'

Kemp shook his head. He drained his cup to the dregs.

'That was clever of you, Venetia, asking me here that night, but it wasn't the first time we'd met. And Carlos Rossi was in the Manor then but not in public view. Neither you nor Vivian could risk that, for by that time you knew who he was... What had he said to you? More importantly, what had he shown you? His birth certificate, his parents' marriage certificate? Does this stuff act quickly by the way?'

The sudden question he shot out had just the effect he desired.

Venetia leaped to her feet with a very unladylike oath. Her untouched coffee stained brown the pale almond-blossom of the Chinese rug as the tray tipped over sending cups, saucers, sugar basin and jugs crashing to the floor.

'Now look what you've done,' said Kemp reprovingly, 'and no servants on hand to clean up the mess.'

It gave him some satisfaction to say the words, although they were the last he was to speak for some time. He remembered settling back on the couch and staring up at the ceiling as Venetia flashed from the room.

The Courtenay arms looked down on him without much interest; they had seen it all before.

AFTERWARDS—how long afterwards he had no idea—he felt tentatively at the lump that had arisen on the back of his head, and knew that the stuff in the coffee had merely been a soporific. It was a heavy blow which had finally knocked him out. He had always disliked Vivian Courtenay but he wouldn't have put it past Venetia to have dealt it herself. Between the two of them he hadn't stood a chance, but then that was just how he had wanted it . . . His murder, on the other hand, would take some time to ar-

range—as had Carlos Rossi's. On that he was taking
a gamble.

Of course he knew exactly where he was. There
was only thin light coming through the vents in the
stone wall, nothing from the grating at the kitchen
end. He groped for his watch but it had gone from
his wrist. He felt in his pockets. Nothing. Even his
handkerchief had been taken. His shirt felt loose at
the neck; well, it hadn't been one of his best ties . . .

He got up painfully from the bare floor on which
he'd been lying. At least he still had his shoes. He
made his way over to where the chinks of fading
daylight filtered into the room. He had neither pen
nor pencil, and nothing to write on anyway. Carlos
Rossi had had nothing, he too had been stripped of
everything except for that screwed-up scrap of paper stuck in the corner of a pocket, or perhaps held
clutched in his fist. No one now would ever know...
But the American had been resourceful; he had noticed those apertures, probably then the sun had been
shining through, and there was one he could reach.

Kemp put his own hand up to that narrow slit,
pushed his fingers through, and waved them about
in the freezing air. When he brought them in they
were blue with cold. He just hoped that John Upshire's minions had strong eyes in the dusk. Calling
out would have been easier, or he might have sung an
appropriate ballad or two, but he was pretty sure the
room had been built to be sound-proof, particularly
to the outside world. Besides, any loud noise would

frighten the rats, and he still had business to do with the human variety now in possession of the Manor.

He crept up the tiny stair, but of course the old iron latch on the door at the top was immovable. Lettice had said the keys had been lost, the door was never locked. It was well and truly locked now. When Rossi had been incarcerated they had probably contrived some temporary barrier on the other side. Kemp wondered what they had told him... That it was a masquerade, a game, some stylish frolic indulged in by the English upper classes? Perhaps at first they had provided for his comfort, fed him and chatted to him, spun him a tale about re-enactment of the legend of the French prisoner... How long before he had begun to shout? There would be no one to hear him, the Elizabethan wing was closed up, even the servants never went near. He could have been there, as Venetia had hinted, the night of the first party...

Anger swelled up in Kemp, blinding his eyes. He struggled against it, came back down the stairs and sat, grasping his knees, hunched up beside the old fireplace. The thing now was to avoid, or at least contain, excess emotion which would be a waste of energy, like draining the fuel tank. He reflected that there was nothing so conducive to deep thought as to be cooped up in a cell with nothing to do. Many of his criminal clients had told him that. He agreed with them now; it concentrated the mind most wonderfully.

He had to think his way through, right into the minds of the twins, to speculate what they would do next...

Of course they could simply leave him there and either pick up the body later when hunger, thirst and cold had done their work, or abandon it to the vermin. But that would be too great a risk; his disappearance, unlike that of the anonymous American, would raise a hue and cry in Newtown. They would know that Lewis Proby must have seen his car going into the drive. Lettice Warrender knew of the secret room, and even in his own office his recent work had linked him with the Courtenay family.

How that galled him still, that deliberate link!

It had been Venetia's doing. It was she who had sought him out to play his part in the devious plot both she and Vivian had thrown themselves into when a terrible truth had been revealed to them by a casual stranger at their gates.

It might at first have been merely a passing encounter, the nicely-spoken young man perhaps asking the way to Ember, and they in their free-and-easy style inviting him in to tea. How long before they had known? Some remark Carlos Rossi had made all unwittingly—for Kemp was sure that Carlos himself had no idea of the truth. That name of Ember... In the old deedbox at Fairlawns Kemp had seen it, passed it by. A younger son had used it once when travelling abroad on the King's business when Cromwell had the power in England.

Charles Courtenay had done the decent thing by that Italian girl in New York. He'd married her, but he would have been afraid to join the family name to such a liaison, he would do what his forebear had done when up to something clandestine. He would use the name of Ember.

But others, too, could have their pride. The girl was ill, perhaps her Italian family blamed him for it. Blanche said they took her away. Charles must have seen the death certificate, for he knew she had died of septicaemia. That could have happened in childbirth... If Rosina had been the well-loved daughter in a close-knit family, the Rossis might not have trusted this English stranger who called himself Charles Ember but they might have wanted Rosina's child, so they never told him.

And all that had happened during the winter of nineteen-forty-six. Carlos had been born to Charles Courtenay and Rosina Rossi nearly a year before the twins' birth; he was the legitimate male heir to the whole of the Courtenay estate, and the chief beneficiary under Silas's will.

Kemp wrapped himself more closely in his jacket. The freezing cold was penetrating his very bones. He knew he had few facts to substantiate the suppositions he was making, and it was only by effort of will and a lot of imagination that he was putting himself into places where others had been, gauging their actions from what he had gleaned of their characters.

But even the most fluid imagination faltered at picturing the scene at Courtenay Manor in the days succeeding the arrival of Carlos. Neither Vivian or Venetia could have been sure at first. Even the remotest possibility that they might lose their inheritance after all these years of waiting, and at the moment of their triumph, must have had an appalling effect on both of them. It sent Venetia flying to her mother, and from that moment Carlos Rossi was doomed. Badgered, as she put it, by her daughter, Blanche said enough to confirm Venetia's worst fears. Blanche herself was told nothing; the knowledge that now quivered between the twins was too dangerous a secret, it clamped them together in deadly conspiracy. Their mother who knew them of old sensed something terrible was about to happen, and distanced herself from them . . .

In his present state Kemp could summon up little enthusiasm for considering Carlos Rossi's actual killing, although he was interested in the timing of it. Carlos had been at the library on August 14, had set off from there to have a look at Ember, and he'd walked straight into a nightmare. Even had he been seen by any of the servants or guests at the Manor, it could only have been a momentary glimpse before he was whisked away for more private hospitality by the twins. And he'd been carrying all his belongings on his back so there would have been no landlady to miss him, no hotel bill left unpaid . . .

From then on, everything was pure conjecture.

They had had over a week to agonize over what should be done—and to contrive their plan. Venetia's plan. Where had they done their talking? Pacing the green drawing-room, drinking in that bleak dining-hall, driving about the countryside? It was their money, of course, that had suborned the others, the lesser breed, the small fry... But it was on Venetia that Kemp concentrated now. Had she sat shredding rose petals on the terrace, tearing at them with frenzied fingers as the ideas within her leapt and multiplied?

It was in her character that it should not be simple. Vivian would have plied the American with drink until he was insensible, then struck a fatal blow on the defenceless skull with a great stone out of the rockery which he would then, quite casually, replace in the soil he owned. Perhaps it had indeed been like that, but it would be she who gave it the classic touch.

If the body had been quite haphazardly cast into some wood or coppice on the estate it would inevitably be found. Although the grounds were supposed to be private little notice had been taken of that in recent years, for Silas had not been one for shooting or the rearing of pheasants. Local lads went after rabbits, ramblers cut corners, and there were always poachers about or farmers with their dogs. No, it would be too great a risk.

'What, in our house?' she would have exclaimed, like Macbeth's lady. 'No, Vivian, we have to be smarter than that. Somewhere, sometime, our precious American will be missed. We don't know who he has already met in Newtown, who he might have told where he was going. We have to make sure the body is found and buried, but not as Carlos Rossi for that would bring inquiries... Inquiries, brother dear, which we cannot afford. I have a better plan.'

Kemp's eyes were closing. He felt light-headed, his thoughts slipping away to the borders of delirium.

She must come soon. He knew she would come. Not to confess—only underlings did that—but to tell him what his fate was, what scheme had been hatched to dispose of him so cleverly that no breath of suspicion could tarnish the Courtenays. He tried desperately to keep awake, though the weakness spreading in his limbs yearned for the ease of unconsciousness.

A light glowed in the kitchen, shone through the grating above his head so that he could see the faint outline of groins in the vaulted roof. He heard the clang of metal in the door-lock, and footsteps on the narrow stair.

She carried a modern table-lamp, trailing its flex behind her. She set it on the ledge of the fireplace and stood looking down on him, her figure grotesquely elongated by its light. He didn't bother to move.

'It ought to be candles,' he said, 'like in a play. You spoil the effect with that sixty-watt bulb.'

He was pleased to see that whatever condition she'd expected to find him in it hadn't been one of sweet humour. At least he hoped it had sounded like sweet humour, though he couldn't be sure, his voice so thin and far away. But it did make her cross.

'You're so stupid. Like all your class. You have no finesse, no style. You never know when to let things be,' she said icily.

He wagged a weak finger at her. A childish gesture. 'Ah, but you chose me, Venetia Proby, because I was stupid.'

She squatted down on the other side of the bricked-up fireplace, her shoes raising a puff of dust from the floor.

'No, Lennox, I chose you because of your reputation.'

'To put two and two together and find a missing husband, dead in a claypit?'

She smiled. 'Something like that. But you were much too slow off the mark. What a nuisance that was. I had to keep popping back to that dirty old caravan site all the time so that I would be there when they came to break the news. Damned inconvenient. But it didn't matter in the end. It was as I had planned.'

'You should have gone to that drama school. You're a loss to the National Theatre.'

'When Vivian and I return from an extensive trip abroad, I may go on the stage. I rather enjoyed my first performance.'

'I should have taken more notice of your legs. I always used to look at the legs of my women clients.

I must be getting old... "Short in the legs," Mrs Carter said, and I ought to have registered it. And Elvira telling me how Mrs Proby knew her way to the washroom...' Kemp kncw he was rambling. His muscles seemed frozen, and he was afraid to move in case they splintered.

Venetia on the other hand was rising gracefully to her feet. She picked up the lamp, coiling the flex round her arm.

'I shall be sorry to see you go, Lennox. It was fun leading you on and you played your part so well. What a pity you got a teensy-weensy bit curious about that very strange American. I'll never know why. Something Lydia Beresford said to you, I suppose. Stupid old woman. I told Vivian to shut her mouth. And I couldn't have anything to do with that. You were holding my hand at the time. Did you think I was about to take you to my bedchamber? Me, Venetia Courtenay?'

The surge of anger warmed the blood in Kemp's veins. He unwound himself from his crouched position. If he threw himself at her when she turned to go up the stair burdened as she was by the lamp, she would be at his mercy. But that was not in the scenario of the play as he had written it, and it was his turn now to write the script.

She must have seen the change in him, sensed his purpose. She was agile and had her wits about her still. With one well-aimed stab from the heel of her

good crocodile shoe she got him in the chest, and
sent him sprawling.

She paused on the bottom step and looked back
disdainfully.

Kemp shook the dust out of his eyes. 'The Sorrentos,' he muttered, 'I've not figured out where they
came into it.'

'We met Alfredo when we were in Sicily once.
Vivian and he got into some brawl in a bistro.' She
shrugged her shoulders. 'Our lawyers got Viv out of
gaol, and Alfredo too. He owed us a favour. It was a
bit of a bore him looking us up when he came here on
holiday, and his family really were the absolute end.
But Alfredo'd sworn undying gratitude, and you
know what the Italians are like.' Kemp winced; he'd
remembered the first time she'd said that. 'And the
brother quite a nice-looking man, with that olive skin
and dark hair—and so very poor. I was reminded of
him...later.' She stopped, then went on more briskly:
'Money, Lennox, people will do anything when they
need the money... And now it's time to put you out
of your misery. You're going to have a nasty car accident on the road back to Newtown. You will be
found drunk, my dear, at the wheel of your car in a
ditch. It's all arranged. You will be dead when they
find you.'

So that was the way it was to be.

This time it had been unequal combat, with the
Courtenays on the losing side. That was what he had
told Inspector Upshire. 'There's no evidence against

them,' he'd said, 'so they have to be caught in the act. They'll use the same *modus operandi* in the second killing...'

'Vivian will come presently,' her voice sang out to him as she unlatched the door at the top of the stairs. 'He's here beside me now with some sort of blunt instrument. Quite appropriate, don't you think, to bring down on the head of a lawyer?'

Kemp wasn't having any of that. He didn't like pain much, and was averse to heroism. If he feigned insensibility it would make Vivian's task easier. He closed his eyes, and went limp on the dusty floor. When he felt the hands at his throat, forcing open his mouth to pour in the fiery spirit, he let his head loll back without protest. Cooking brandy, he thought with disgust. They might at least have made it something decent. They can well afford it.

He was dragged from the room, his limbs stretched and racked as he was bundled up the stone steps, across the kitchen and down the passageway where he had been so gaily led by Lettice on the night of the fireworks. There were rockets now, too, exploding in his brain like coloured stars as he felt himself carried by both the Courtenay twins out to his car.

It was only then, in the driveway, that Vivian hit him with something and Kemp passed out.

'Was that really necessary?' Venetia called out from the terrace. Vivian was standing beside Kemp's car looking down at the inert form at his feet.

'Of course it was,' he shouted back. 'We'd never get him into the driving seat otherwise. Once we get him in, I'll do the steering ... You'll have to come with me, Sis, as you did when we got rid of Rossi.'

Venetia came running. 'I had to get the things for his pockets,' she said, her breath coming short and misting the freezing air, 'and make sure nothing was left. I wonder what made him come meddling into our affairs? Could it have been the Sorrentos, after all the trouble we went to? I thought that family as safe as money could buy... Well, Mr Lennox Kemp will be found dead, an unfortunate victim of his own folly. We dined and wined him too well... Who said murder once done could never be repeated? We've done it, brother of my heart, we've done it!'

She was exultant, her voice and her silvery laugh echoing high across the still, cold night.

Vivian had opened the car doors.

'Then let's get this fool into his car, and we'll finish him off when we dump it,' he said gruffly. 'It was a hell of a lot easier with Rossi... At least he was dead before we got him to the claypit.'

LIKE AVENGING ANGELS the shadows rose from behind every bush, the men of Upshire's force. He himself climbed slowly from the back seat of Kemp's car where he had been lying, cramped, and growing more and more irritable by the hour.

'Mr Vivian Courtenay? Mrs Venetia Proby? I am Chief Inspector Upshire of the Newtown Police. I must ask you to accompany us to the station to answer inquiries into the disappearance of Carlos Ember Rossi...'

ARCHIE GILLORN glanced ironically at the livid scar on Kemp's forehead.

'Dear me,' he said, 'Chancery must have become more dangerous since my time. It was always considered a safe field in which to practise...'

'Not when there are undomesticated animals about,' said Kemp, 'but I came here to report to the trustees.'

Archie looked inquiringly at Arnold Crayshaw, who nodded that the senior man should do the talking. Archie spoke slowly, and with some relish.

'By the death of Silas Courtenay the whole legal estate and most of the beneficial interest passed to the legal heir. I understand he has been checked out?'

'Impeccable credentials,' said Kemp, 'confirmed with the help of the New York Police Department, and the International Genealogical Index kept, as you are aware, by the Mormons. Pity Carlos didn't consult them in the first place,' he added as an aside, 'but of course he wasn't seeking either a family or a fortune...'

'Let me continue,' said Archie. 'In olden times on failure of heirs, the Crown could claim by escheat. That has been abolished, but as Carlos Rossi was legally entitled to the property at the moment of his death and he died intestate and without heirs...'

'Who said he did?' Kemp couldn't stop himself smiling. 'Carlos Rossi was married and a good family man. He left a proper will: Everything of which he died possessed—which he thought meant the contents of his haversack and a fifth share in his papa's restaurant—to go to his wife Emelia to be held on trust for his twin sons, Peter and Paul. There are two little boys in Brooklyn who have no idea what's coming to them . . .'

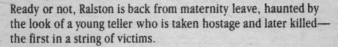

BARBARA PAUL
IN-LaWS
aNd OUtLAWs

Gillian Clifford, once a Decker in-law, returns to the family fold
to comfort Raymond's widow, Connie. Clearly, the family is
worried. Who hates the Deckers enough to kill them?

And as the truth behind the murder becomes shockingly clear,
Gillian realizes that once a Decker, always a Decker—a position she's discovering can be most precarious indeed.

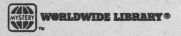

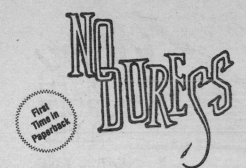

First Time in Paperback

MIRIAM BORGENICHT

A tragedy turns into a living nightmare when health counselor Linda Stewart's adopted infant daughter is legally reclaimed by the baby's natural teenage mother— and both are found dead two days later.

Linda's agonizing grief is channeled into a burning determination to solve these senseless murders. While suspicions of drug involvement might explain the sudden fortune the young mother had acquired, Linda's subtle probing takes a seedy turn into black-market adoptions.

"Borgenicht's perceptive comments on troubling social issues generate plenty of tension." —Publishers Weekly

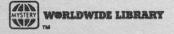

Mom DOTH MURDER SLEEP

James Yaffe

First Time in Paperback

As chief investigator for the Mesa Grande, Colorado, public defender's office, Dave's reputation for solving the toughest cases had followed him all the way from New York City. So had his mother, his very unofficial homicide consultant. She did her best detective work over plates of pot roast and strudel, happily feeding her son while gleaning all the details of his latest case.

Now murder takes center stage at a local amateur theater production of *Macbeth*. Mom, of course, has some ideas of her own about whodunit as dark secrets, stormy passions, rage and jealousy unfold.

"Mom's detective style is the cream of a rich detective mystery."
—*The Drood Review of Mystery*

WORLDWIDE LIBRARY
TM